ANOTHER MAN'S OFFICE

Penelope Trevor

ALLEN & UNWIN

The author and publishers would like to thank the following for use of copyright material: Lyrics from the song 'Cats in the Cradle' (p. 166) by Harry Chapin/Sandy Chapin. Reproduced by permission of Warner/Chappell Music Australia Pty Ltd. Unauthorised reproduction is illegal.

First published in 2000

Allen & Unwin
9 Atchison Street
St Leonards NSW 2065
Australia
Phone: (61 2) 8425 0100
Fax: (61 2) 9906 2218
Email: frontdesk@allen-unwin.com.au
Web: http://www.allen-unwin.com.au

National Library of Australia
Cataloguing-in-Publication entry:

Trevor, Penelope, 1960– .
Another man's office.

ISBN 1 86508 323 2.

I. Title.

A823.3

Set in 11.5/14 pt Adobe Garamond by DOCUPRO, Sydney
Printed by Australian Print Group, Maryborough, Victoria

10 9 8 7 6 5 4 3 2 1

To my mother, Marie Trevor, who stopped me burning the manuscript at the end of one very long year.
As she says, growing wings is hard.

ACKNOWLEDGMENTS

Thanks to Peter Bishop I was granted a fellowship at Varuna Writers Centre in 1997. The support was invaluable, and the uninterrupted time allowed me to find the shape of the novel.

Research and editorial

Thanks to Myint Myint San and Soe Soe for their guidance on the political and social realities of life in Burma, as well as their courage and trust in sharing a little of their own story. Also to Myint Myint San for her editorial eye regarding all matters Burmese. To Susan Menzies and Nyi Khwat Joom Ong, again for their bravery and trust in sharing their personal experiences with me. To Carmel Elliot for her efficiency and enthusiasm regarding military protocol and research. To David Christianson and Sonia from the Odiyana Centre regarding the intricacies, political and theoretical, of Tibetan Buddhism. I would also like to acknowledge the monks, nuns and members of the Western sanga with whom I lived in Nepal. Thanks also to Sophie Cunningham for her ongoing support and faith in the project. And Patricia Hepworth for her astute feedback, and her intuitive powers of deduction regarding my spelling. Finally I would like to give big thanks for the delicate eye of my editor Beverly McDonald.

Community funding

I would like to acknowledge the following people without whom I could never have written this book: Ian Brealey for his gift of a computer without which my career as a writer would have been seriously challenged; Prudence Holt and Kevin Burnett of Red Falcon Design for their fortnightly gift of veggies that kept my children from developing scabies; Pauline and Jack McCarthy for their financial and other support; Jeff Doveton for his skills as a computer sharp-shooter, and his patience with the technologically challenged; John Street Community Child Care Cooperative for child and parent care above and beyond the call of duty; and again I would like to thank Beverly McDonald for keeping the electricity running.

THE PAST

Two men's eyes meet across a line of war. Neither knows why he does not pull the trigger. The bamboo groans, and the monsoon rain keeps falling.

Twenty-two years later one man is dead, his son, Wana, in prison. The other blind, his son, Tim, a disappointment.

Burma, 1985

Wana,

sits on the edge of a metal sleeping bunk in an isolation cell in Insein prison. He sits with his back straight, his hands resting on his knees, his feet flat on the floor. The prison is silent, everyone knows what is about to happen. Even the rats.

The soldiers come. Wana follows the sound of their booted step to cell fifteen. Hears the wind chime ring of keys. The drop of the turning of the lock and the weighted squeak of the cell door opening. Each sound clean against the silence.

Accusations are levelled at the prisoner of cell fifteen. Bald statements of treason and conspiracy to incite social unrest. The prisoner is asked to account for himself.

There is no reply.

He is ordered to account for himself. To name others.

He does not.

He is encouraged with a fist to the gut.

Wana bites down on anger as sounds are forced from his friend, the prisoner in cell fifteen.

Sounds but no words. And so he's hit again.

Tears run down Wana's cheeks.

From the end cell a single voice climbs in defiance.

'Don't let your smile go.
There will never be a permanent defeat.
Holding together, we are united . . .'

Song breaks the spell of isolation. Another voice joins the first, and another.

'And the blood in our hearts is radiant and red.
Our hands that make the history
Are ready for the sake of freedom . . .'

Voices circling like birds fill the prison, soar above the sounds of impact. Wana remembers why he is here. Song stirs his heart to hope. He frees his voice to rise circling with the others.

'Students be united! . . .'

Their song drowns out the squeaking orders of flustered guards. Wana feels himself smile.

The moment is cut by a cry. An open-mouthed howl. The word 'freedom' drops from Wana's lips unvoiced. Cold runs through him. There is no trace of his friend in that sound. There's only an animal in pain.

A guard laughs. They stopped the singing.

The execution which follows is swift. His friend is dragged out into the courtyard. A shot rings out. Wana's body jumps. One bullet to the back of the head is a traitor's death. His friend was not a traitor, he was a good man.

In the silence that follows Wana knows he is going to die. His time is coming. Until this day he hadn't really believed it. He wishes he could have seen his son, Aik, just once; hopes his death will have some meaning; that things will change; that life will be better. He wonders if you can be proud of a father who never held you.

Wana takes a deep breath. He likes the sensation. Likes the way the air moves through his lungs. His father was a soldier. He's glad his father did not live to see the soldiers turn against the people.

Four hundred and twenty-six miles away,
outside the small village of Pegan, Tim pedals a hired bicycle down a manicured dirt road. Dust stirs in the too warm air. Birds caw. Tim looks up. The sky is tinged with pink. The underbelly of each cloud illuminated, as the heat of the day strikes the promised cool of evening. Tim breathes in deep.

'Everything in Burma is nice.'
That's what the manager at the hotel he's staying at said, and Tim thinks perhaps he's right.

Drawn to Burma, on a kind of pilgrimage. To see the remains of a once Buddhist kingdom, a handful of forgotten temples. Built of stone. Built to last. Unlike the palaces, which were built of wood and have long since washed away, splinters in the rain, as was intended. Tim has, for the past three days run his fingers across ancient carvings, meditated on impermanence, and eaten mango. In Rangoon he ate lobster.

Lunch at the Strand was 'a must' when in Burma. Or so he'd been told. Along with the black market sale of duty free cigarettes and scotch, although he still isn't quite sure why this is 'a must', since every cent he spends while he's here 'must' be entered into a small book stapled to his passport, along with the receipts for money officially changed. And apparently the two must tally.

—Bureaucracy.

The word reminds Tim of his father.

—'Mum! Dad! I sold the car you gave me and bought a ticket for India.'

His father looked like he'd just been shot. That had been nine months ago. They haven't spoken since. Tim's written once. Told his parents he's a Buddhist now. That he's found what he was looking for. His mother sent a letter 'Poste Restante', said she was happy for him. Didn't mention his father.

Tim lets his eyes run the length of corn on his left. A stupa crowns the field. He stops the bike. Walks it to the side of the road. Leans it against a stunted tree. Makes his way around the field.

The stupa is simpler than most, smaller. Like some strange ripe fruit. Tim peers inside. There is a fetid odour. He takes a few tentative steps down the tunnel. His eyes adjust. The chamber in the centre is lit by shafts of light that come from the ceiling. Cut across the dark. He can't see what else is there.

As Tim steps out into the central chamber, bats beat the air with leathered wings. He ducks. Covers his head. Nothing comes for him. The bats seem to settle. He lowers his arms. A thirty-foot Buddha, carved out of a single piece of black garnet, looks down on him. Perfectly crafted, the face seems almost real. Tim smiles. He's found a treasure. He wishes his father could understand. The Dharma is bigger than the artist. Tim was an artist so he understands.

He runs his hand across the smooth stone of the Buddha's knee, cool despite the heat. Steps back to take in its beauty. His breath catches. The throat and the heart are eaten away. There is a cancer. Tim backs out of the stupa. Catches his retreat as he hits the light.

Crows call. Tim feels a little stupid, his heart beats too fast. He looks around. The field and the road are deserted. No-one has seen. He heads towards the stunted tree the bike leans against. The cancer threw him.

THE PRESENT

Fifteen years later

—*Quiet. Very quiet.*

The words are in Tim's head. He's not conscious yet.

'Argh,' the sound escapes his lips.

His eyelids flutter, small movements, lighter than the wings of a moth. There is the smell of urine. His eyes open. Black. There is only black. He blinks, slowly. The black registers. His eyes are open and he can't see. Jesus he can't see. Panic rises in his gut. Not because of the situation; he hasn't even got to that yet. Just that he can't see. Like his father, the Captain, he can't see. His stomach knots.

Caught in the margin between conscious and unconscious, Tim reasons he must be dreaming. Tells himself his eyes aren't really open. That if he could just open them everything would be alright!

But they are open. They're open and he can't see!

Fear, a tourniquet of fine, red tangled line cuts the flow of air to his lungs. His heart, engorged with stale blood, hurts.

—Breathe!

The voice in his head is his only reason. He makes himself breathe.

There is a scratching in the dark. Images of being eaten alive, by unseen things, fill his mind.

—Dreaming.

Nightmare dreaming, he tells himself.

—Just a nightmare.

—Don't be ridiculous!

The other voice in his head is his father's.

—Look! Really look.

Tim remembers his father holding him firm by the scruff of the neck, making him look until he saw the snake coiled in the grass. He'd always wondered how his father had known it was there.

Tim strains to see; tries to separate shadow from black. The scratching stops. Suddenly there is movement. Black moving through black. A shadow form.

—A rat!

He can see it.

—A rat! Yes, a rat!

He's not blind. It's his father who's blind. And he's not dreaming. It's just dark. Very dark. Tim's head begins to clear.

In coming to full consciousness there is a beat without thought. He blinks. The rat moves. He tries to keep track of it. Moves his head. Pain knifes his skull, shoots through his right shoulder.

'Shiiit,' his word is choked.

He's tied, trussed like a pig on his side.

Awake now, it comes back, all of it; the local bus, a jeep with a tarp roof; the jungle; the afternoon, warm, damp, capped with a grey-weighted sky; monsoon clouds, glimpsed rising like demons above the escarpments of valleys, where rice fields shimmer fluorescent in stolen shafts of afternoon sun; and then back into the jungle, submerged in a sea of green that pitches itself against the sky; the toothless woman next to him, her cocks caged in cane; the two children opposite, eating chicken, pink and charred; a sudden jolt; the sound of worn brakes, steel against steel shooting through him like fingernails on a blackboard; everything flung; one of the children hits her head, heavy red drops on her white blouse.

Tim remembers bending down to help her. Being hauled backwards out of the jeep and thrown onto the ground. Looking up at soldiers, faces covered, eyes framed in cloth. He remembers trying to stand, and the crack of a rifle coming down on his skull. Everything had bled then, sound and vision, one into another. Into a sickening heat that rose within him. That's the last thing Tim remembers, and his head hurts worse for remembering.

—This can't be happening. Not to me!

His thought is a scream, filled with panic. His gut knots. His ears fill with the sound of his own blood, deafening.

He tries to kick out. Fight against the ropes that bind him. They tighten. Cut into his wrists and ankles. Face down in the dirt, twisted and hurting, tears run across the bridge of Tim's nose.

Breathe, he tells himself, breathe. Boys don't cry.

In the dark, tied like an animal, Tim tries to think clearly, unravel his fear in question and answer.

—Who would have done this? And why?

—Why me?

No, he can't think about that now. That's a different kind of question. One he can't answer. He makes himself breathe in to the count of three, out to the count of three. Controls the racing of his heart. He remembers all the rumours he's heard about Northern Thailand. But that was to do with the heroin trade and he had nothing to do with hard drugs. Never had, never would. He'd seen *Midnight Express.* Besides opium was a black drug. All too dangerous. He can't imagine his timing could have been so bad as to land him in the wrong place at the wrong time.

—Maybe they think I'm someone else. A courier. A dealer.

Tim's mind races with the possibilities.

—Don't be ridiculous!

—If this was over drugs I'd be dead.

He vaguely remembers hearing there'd been some trouble on the Thai–Burmese border earlier in the year.

—In the refugee camps.

But what did that have to do with him? He'd been to Burma once, that was it, and the refugee camps were miles from where he'd been headed. At least he thinks they were.

He'd been looking for the monks who live in the jungle like the Buddha. He'd been told if he got off the bus where a cliff catacombed with carved shrines forces the road to the right, he'd find the monks, or at least they'd find him.

—But I never got there.

—Hostage.

The word fills him. Face down in the dark, that's how it is. Snapshots of his life counterpoint sharp in his mind, against the smell of foreign soil lodged in his nostrils.

'Don't go Tim. Not this time.' Vera's eyes are angry.

'Christmas! His birthday! You're never around. Mischa's not going to tell you but he's hurt.'

Tim's jaw tightens with the memory. He thinks she'd be laughing now, imagines her smile and all its unspoken words.

—'I told you not to go. Life catches us all.'

Well fuck her. Mischa'd been fine about him going. He'd told Mischa he'd stay if he wanted him to and Mischa'd said, 'No Dad. Go! Really.'

A snapshot from the airport. He and Mischa are saying goodbye. Mischa's hair is sun golden. Threads, between his fingers. Vera, standing with her two other children, claims Mischa with her eyes. He is her eldest. Mischa looks up at Tim. His eyes are ocean blue, tinged with channels of green.

—Loves the sea.

—That's where I'll take him when I get home.

The rat sniffs at Tim's feet.

—Home. Two more weeks and I'd have been home.

A fissure opens in the granite of his heart. Tim roars.

'I am on my way home!'

Mischa wakes thinking about his Dad.

Missing him. The feeling sticks all day, in a kind of back of the head way. Until he finds himself hanging upside down in the apple tree, in the front garden, waiting for the mail.

He hopes Vera doesn't notice. Tim's not much of a letter writer, and Mischa doesn't really think there'll be anything. It's just sort of where he ended up, in case. He doesn't want his Mum to be angry with his Dad.

Petals of purple swim across the grass, strange fish in an alien sea. The world looks better to Mischa upside down. When Tim gets back, they'll go to the beach.

In the kitchen Vera stirs soup. She knows where Mischa is, in the front yard, waiting. She'd like to punch Tim in the nose. Her feelings are too much for the pot. It spits.

'Damn!'

She runs her wrist under cold water.

Gentle, she tells herself, and begins again. She lifts a single kidney bean to her lips on the end of the old wooden spoon. Cautions herself against letting her mind throw up thoughts of Tim. It turns the food bitter. She hears Mischa's voice, light, a thin line against the mail man's. There's no letter.

'Fuck you Tim,' she mutters.

Exhausted,

face down in the dirt, labouring for breath, his own sweat salting the sting of rope biting into his wrists and ankles, Tim understands what it really means to be bound against your will. It's fucking awful.

His memory catches on images stored from the world's news; a Romanian child, an orphan, 'I'm scared,' he says, his face covered in sores; a woman raped by soldiers shakes her head, 'It's wrong,' she says, 'that they can do this'; a hungry man says, 'Things are bad. Really bad'. Tim never understood before how carefully you had to listen. That the worse things are the less there is to say.

Reduction, he thinks, to reduce something to its

simplest state; to weaken; to survive. Stories tumble into him, real now. People's lives. His lungs hurt with every breath.

Outside he hears voices. His consciousness is raw. He's all ears.

—Know thy enemy.

His father's voice is in his head.

He's straining to hear. To make out a word, a familiar syllable. To have some knowledge. Torchlight illuminates the crack between door and floor. He has a sense of distance.

—Five feet maybe.

The door is thrown open. Light blinds him. Too much, too soon. Everything happens quickly then; two men roll him over; cut the rope between his wrists and ankles; his legs fall flat, straighten, cramp.

'Fuuuck.'

The word is rolled out on his breath as he curls in a ball on the floor, knees pulled to his chin to loosen the cramp. He is hauled to sit by the back of his shirt. He struggles. Hits out. Grinds words to grit, behind clenched teeth. He can't stand being manhandled.

He is forced to sit, back flat, against a rotten timber wall. Defiant, he stares into the light shone at his face. The man in the doorway is veiled by light. A silhouette. Feet apart, one hand behind his back.

—A military man.

Tim's father stands like that. Now Tim knows there's been a mistake.

—They've got the wrong man.

Hope dances. The child in a man's breast.

'Yo . . .'

His throat is blocked with dirt and mucus. He coughs. Spits. Deepens his voice, begins again.

'I think you've got the wrong man,' he says.

And he tries to smile as though this is no big deal. Can easily be sorted out.

Contempt escapes on the breath of the soldier in the doorway. The hairs on the back of Tim's neck rise. The soldier barks an order. Quickly the others leave. Scared rabbits. Tim feels a rush of adrenalin prepare him. He holds his ground. Keeps his gaze even. It's instinct. Like two dogs from different packs, they stare each other down.

The soldier laughs as though the confrontation were amusing, but only slightly. He turns and leaves. Shuts out the light. Bolts Tim back into darkness. Voices recede into silence.

Tim begins to shake. He eyed the enemy, held his ground, was outside himself. He played the game. And it had come naturally. Suddenly Tim remembers the smell of his father too close.

—Damn him!

All those bloody games in the backyard when he was a child, they've left their mark.

—But this isn't a game.

Tim's stomach turns, he dry retches in the dark. His bile underlines the silent cry.

—How can this be happening to me?

He clenches his jaw against fear.

'Meditate,' he tells himself. 'Meditate. Breathe.'

Tim tries to empty his mind. Dissolve his fear and the walls around him by building a visualisation. He follows the instructions step by step. Visualises the Buddha in the likeness of his teacher. His teacher's not so perfect, but that's how you're supposed to do it. Tim struggles with devotion these days. Breathing in, breathing out. He lets the issue go. Dedicates his meditation for the benefit of sentient beings. Tries to feel it, not just think it. Makes himself include the soldiers. Then he visualises white light washing through him, carrying away the darkness, the black of his sins.

Rimpoche, his teacher, calls the black 'negative emotion'. Tim still thinks in terms of sin.

Slowly his body absorbs the adrenalin pumping through him, and the shaking stops. He is in the pure land of his own imagining. He is safe here. There is a gentle wind. Mantra protects him from too many thoughts.

Captain Rhyder strides,

down what he knows to be the clean, neatly swept path, from the military academy. He can feel the sun on his back. Imagines a blue sky. He remembers blue. Cadets pass.

'Sir.'

The Captain nods. Raises his eyebrows in recognition in case any of them are his students. If they're not they won't notice, if they are it'll throw them. They'll think he recognised their voices. Strategy, the Captain smiles to himself. That's why the army still had a use for him, because of his exceptional strategic ability. The money they spent on his education was not wasted.

He strides the three blocks and thirty-seven steps to his house with more confidence than a sighted man. Less distraction. Slowing only as he approaches the front gate.

She's at the letterbox. It's the way she closes it, the sound, the postman's hand is heavier. The Captain knows what she's hoping for but his son won't have written. He doesn't understand why she still bothers to look. He'd have thought, after fifteen years, she'd have learnt that their son's slanty-eyed beliefs in renunciation included the small things. Courtesies, like remembering birthdays. He walks past her without a word.

The Captain imagines their house is white, no-one's ever told him this. Sighted people don't realise how much information they never think to share. The keys are in his pocket, marked for touch, but the front door is open.

Inside it is quiet, still, dead and ordered. He sits at his desk. He's got some calls to make. The woman who smells of lilies. She wants to make a documentary. Open people's eyes to the world of the blind, inspire independence, a notion of equality.

—Stupid bitch.

Beneath the lilies he'd smelt pheromones. She wanted to fuck him. He was still a good-looking man. He worked at it. The army wanted the PR. He was a shining example of rehabilitation. A civilian now, a consulting lecturer. Captain was an honorary title. And he hates the cool, ordered house his wife keeps so well for him. So that his blindness slips almost unnoticed into their daily lives, enabling him to be the blind man he is. Exceptional in his normality.

Dissolving into nothingness,

the complex layers of Tim's visualisation leave him, and for a heartbeat he rests in emptiness. There is no fear without thought but the mind is a restless child.

—Political.

The word fills him.

—I am a political prisoner.

For Tim the realisation holds a poetic irony. He's never been political. Never been able to understand the carving up of continents into countries, the greed of politicians, the blood lust of soldiers. *The Little Prince* is his political bible. He read it first when he was eleven.

Memory colours the thought. For years he kept his opinions to himself. Out of respect for his father, the Captain, who lost his sight patrolling one of those lines that cut continents into countries. It wasn't until he was a teenager that silence became a problem.

Tim remembers the white-blue of a dry, forty-degree day. The smell of rotting jacaranda leaves in the gutter of the garage, making him gag, and the tight place in his gut that was anger. His father was yelling. So the whole neighbourhood could hear.

> 'Don't tell me it's too hot. You're not going to last five minutes in the army. You sound like a girl. A bit of honest work might make a man out of you. Which'd be a bloody miracle.'

Tim tries to let go of the memory. It still hurts.

He can't. Memory becomes physical. He feels the tight place inside giving way, with the rush of a sea wall collapsing. Knows he was down off the roof in seconds, confronting his father. Telling him what he really thought about his stupid army and his stupid war.

His father hit him then. Tim remembers the sting of the slap. And catching the impulse to hit back. Catching it because his father was blind.

—I should have hit back.

Tim doesn't know where the thought comes from. He just

knows it's true. His head hurts. 'Sore' he thinks is a very sad word.

'Fuck. I don't like this. I'll go crazy locked up.'
A voice in Tim's head tells him people do. He smiles to himself. The rat emerges scratching in the corner.

'A political prisoner. I've never even voted.'
His tongue drags dry on the roof of his mouth.

—Maybe I should have.
It's just a thought. It doesn't go anywhere.

Tim needs to move. Stretch out his legs. He hesitates. As a boy he had to steel himself before uncurling his legs into the cool unknown of the bed. Some things don't change. Fear has an edge.

—Give into it and reason ceases.

—A boy, not a man.
The voices in his head speak in tongues.

Panic rises. He's not prepared for this. He's not equipped and the air is filled with ghosts. Thin hungry ghosts, that suck on his plump flesh, hold him down and rub their memories across his unprotected mind. Dark images of loss and labour and silenced screams.

Tim feels what it would be to never see Mischa again, feels the cauterising of his heart. Old voices tell him it's his own fault. That he is careless. Lazy. Christian voices that use the tone of his father.

Tim kicks out, thrashes. If he wants to hard enough he can break these ropes. But he can't, the ropes hold. His wrists begin to bleed and his heart labours in his chest, a dinosaur of a thing, until anger sits in his gut, heavy as unbaked dough.

—Enough!
His body shuts his mind down. He's tired, very tired.

He leans back against the wall and lets his eyes close. His body is summoning the little death, sleep. Tim free-falls. An image stamped fluorescent across the open night of his mind catches him. Water and a yellow rose. Not thin and lemon. But cadmium.

—A yellow rose?

He turns the flower in his mind. The one he picked for Vera, through the wrought iron fence of the Embassy their last night in Delhi, more than a decade ago.

They fucked all night. In the morning, he cupped the swollen lips of her vagina in his hand, beautiful. She cried. He caught the seven-fifteen bus and didn't really think about her again until he came home, three months later, and she picked him up from the airport.

—Arcing time.

The words come into his head and the definition.

—The interval between the parting of the arcing contacts and the extension of the arc.

He knows the feeling of interval.

Thinks of Vera in bed with Joe. How they would both be curled one into the other. The house quiet. The children, Mischa, sleeping. And he wonders if she still thinks of him. He wishes he'd written.

—Written.

The word brings with it the remembered image of nipple pink envelopes, the kind his mother uses. He hasn't written to her either. He meant to. For her birthday. But he got caught up.

The last time he saw her, a year, eighteen months ago, she made him coffee, there were lamingtons. Coconut got stuck between his teeth. He can't remember what they talked about. The harder he tries, the emptier that afternoon seems, like a perfectly ironed white tablecloth; not a mark.

—Still I should have written. Just sent a card.

He imagines her checking the letterbox. Feels her disappointment.

—She won't say anything.

—No. She'll just bundle the oversight up with the rest.

—Packages of ten, tied with string.

—Martyr.

—She makes a good martyr.

Tim opens his eyes. He didn't know he felt like that about his mother.

In the strange quiet of dark, without reference, Tim wonders for the first time when his mother became the things she did; the clean house, the apron, the lamingtons. It's not just that he grew up, there's something else.

The memory's in his groin. It happened when he understood.

He is twelve, they are at a barbecue. He's been playing hide'n'seek under the house, in the dark, with Susie Quin. So when he sees his father run his hand along the arm of a woman, and slip his fingers beneath the short bell sleeve of her dress, he understands. He remembers feeling his mother watching from across the garden. Looking at her and blushing. That's when it happened. All the colour drained from her face. And she dissolved backwards into herself until she wasn't there any more.

Tim replays the memory.

Flashes on her face in the car driving home. She wouldn't look at him. Kept her eyes on the road.

—Didn't want to talk about it.

—Who would?

—I would.

He thinks he's feeling his mother's pain.

'Fuck him!'

The anger is his.

Tim suddenly realises how different they are, he and his mother. She didn't want to talk. Didn't see the point.

—She was always going to stay.

There's his answer. Truth rests like a stone on the bed of a river. It's just how it is. He wonders why she'd stay.

—Love.

That's what she'd say.

—Pity.

That's what he'd like to think. Neither's right. It's more complicated than that.

—Loyalty. She's very loyal.

—Like a dog.

Tim flinches at his own cynicism. Sometimes he really can be a bastard. She's loyal to him too. Never says a word against him.

—Can't. Doesn't talk.

Tim now sees that for his mother talking's dangerous. If she talks to him, he'll use what she says against his father. If she talks to his father he'll use what she says against him. Tim's never seen before the thin margin they leave for her between them.

He feels slightly sick. It's his father who's the bastard. He's the one that fucks around. Who uses his blindness as licence to touch women.

Tim remembers the first time he took Vera home to meet his parents, the way his father touched her, felt the strength of her.

—And she let him.

—Because he's blind.

—Yeah! Because he's fucking blind!

—'So that's why you always make love with the light on. So you don't feel like him.'

Vera is in his head. Looking up at him from beneath a mass of tousled hair.

She is the only one who has ever noticed.

'Come on, it'll be alright,' she'd said and turned off the light. Put his hand between her legs. And he smelt her.

—Breathe.

He tells himself.

—Breathe.

The images are too strong. Hallucinations more than thoughts.

Bound in the dark there is no distraction from oneself. The pitch of Tim's pain and discomfort grows. His mind treads too close to scenes of violation.

—NO!

He cuts the image. Breathes fast and deep.

'Keep busy. Keep my mind busy,' he whispers.

He's read *Papillon*.

—Gotta keep my mind busy.

Tim's body aches. His arms, tied behind his back, pull his shoulders to pinch on his spine.

—Relieve the pain.

—Work to release it, let it go.

He rolls his head. Imagines each vertebra lengthening. Lifts his shoulders, breathes into them. It doesn't work. The pain is in his bones, sharp, reaching for his skull. Fear lifts bile to seep bitter into the back of his throat.

—Escape.

That's what he's got to do. Escape.

—How?

He can't. His hands are tied behind his back, his feet bound.

—Houdini!

Tim remembers he wore a red cape. A black and white film, but a red cape. He rolls onto his side. Imagines he's Houdini. Curls small, thinks his arms loose in their sockets. He'll slip his tied wrists beneath him, slide them out along the length of his legs. Pop them over his toes. And look down on his tied wrists. It's the first step. Then he'll work out what to do next. Tim recognises that now he's thinking it feels better.

Trying to get his tied wrists to slip beneath his bottom is not as easy as he'd imagined. He turns circles in the dirt, coats himself. Sweat runs along the creases of his knees and elbows, itches at his hairline. He can't do it. His back is longer than his arms.

He rests. The sound of his breath loud, rasping in the silence.

—Some Houdini.

And suddenly he gets it.

—Arch the other way.

Logic is freedom.

Tim arches backwards, tries to turn himself inside out. His right thigh cramps.

'Jesus!'

He kicks out straight.

—Salt. Should eat more salt.

The knack of getting his arms from the back of him to the front is all-absorbing. The structural manipulation.

Tim tries again and again, arching, willing his body to lengthen and loosen.

Arching rolls him onto his back. His head takes his weight. He works his bound wrists beneath his bottom. But when he tries to move them forward, up the length of his legs, he can't. He collapses. He can see it in his mind, how his body has to move to make it possible. He has to flip his legs out of the arch and back over his head, straight like a gymnast, not crumple in on himself. Tim rolls onto his side to rest.

Beneath the door is a line of weak dawn light. He stares. Light changes everything. He struggles to sit.

As Tim watches the light strengthens. Pushes under the door and splays across the floor, illuminating the dimensions of his confinement.

—Like magic.

He feels for the first time what it would be like to be really blind, like his father. Locked forever in a world of remembered images. He thinks he will be sick. He never understood before.

'It'd be horrible.'

The words dribble from his lips. Understanding is a physical sensation.

His father had been a physical man in his prime when he lost his sight. At forty-one Tim knows what it is to be past your prime. Men understand. Women don't. They laugh and say things like, 'you're only as old as you feel', or 'ever heard the saying, old before your time?' They don't know what it feels like, the waning of the bull in the blood.

There'd be times travelling when he'd meet up with others, younger men, eager to pick his brains about where to go. At first they were respectful. Even a little deferential but as the night went on there'd always be a scratching and scenting beneath the camaraderie. Arm wrestles, midnight swims out past the breakwater, something. Tim would withdraw then, it was instinct.

The part that made him smile was the irony of women. He had a lot more women now he was older. Some woman would always follow him down the beach, saying she knew exactly how he felt and then with the moonlight reflected in her eyes, would circumnavigate the universe with liquid philosophy, while he watched the way she arched her back, his feet firmly planted on the ground, his cock getting hard.

Is that how it had been for his father after the accident, the recompense for having lost his sight? Is that why he flaunted it, even in front of his wife? Tim has never thought like this before. About his father as a man. About himself as a man.

Tim's mind makes pictures; his father aged twenty-four, golden haired, leading men through the chaos of jungle and green. Tim imagines a young corporal, a mate, reaching out to brush away a tangle of hanging vine, home to a grenade. Out of the corner of his eye his father sees a dull patch, his eyesight's sharp. The rest is instinct. He knocks the young soldier backwards with the butt of his rifle, grabs the grenade with his left hand, hurls it awkwardly. The jungle thwarts him. The grenade explodes, sending up dirt and needles of jungle shrapnel. When the Captain takes his hands from his face he cannot see.

Tim stares at the hard packed dirt floor, in the light he can see every detail. His eyes begin to close, exhaustion is stealing him from consciousness, jumbling thoughts and images; his father Captain Rhyder, uniforms and medals, and Vera's breasts. Mischa.

The Captain knows it's late.

At his front door he stops and feels for the time, four-fifty. Friday, he thinks, Freya's day, named after the Goddess of Love. He feels the breath of dawn on his cheek, smiles to himself. The Captain has the smell of lilies about him.

Palming his key, he slips it smoothly into the lock and admits himself into his neat and ordered home without a sound.

In the bathroom, he thinks about showering. His wife is sleeping. He pictures her lying on her side, her belly relaxed. The picture in his head is of her belly, soft with age, filling his hand as he takes her from behind. The lady of the lilies rode him, let him taste her, explore her, performed for him with her tight muscles and firm skin. He'd felt her cervix, hard, masculine, a womb barred from seed, no problems there. Sex is as close as he gets to an adrenalin rush these days, Jesus he misses it. But a cunt empty of heart leaves a sad taste in his mouth. His edges are softening.

He slips into bed next to his wife. Her back turned against him, against his constant betrayals. He works his hand beneath the tangle of her cotton nightshirt and cups her soft belly. She doesn't stir. He hardens against her, rides gently between her buttocks, she rises slightly. She'll deny it in the morning. He pushes into her warmth, gentle. Home, he falls asleep.

The rat is at Tim's ankle, sniffing.

A whisker traces a line across the bridge of his foot. Suddenly awake, he kicks out. The rat scurries. The pieces of his consciousness settle around his racing heart.

Bang, the door flies open. There's a soldier with a gun, his face cloaked. Two other soldiers push past him. They have knives. Tim is dragged to his feet, all the air goes out of him.

—Gutted, like a stuck pig.

Is a thought.

The ropes at his ankles and wrists are cut. He is dragged roughly to stand, his wrists cuffed in front of him. He almost laughs.

'Guess Houdini had a key,' he says.

They don't get the joke. They leave.

The cuffs are stained with rust. Other men's sweat has greased them. Tim stares at the open door, at the soldier with his gun, beyond him it's green, beautiful.

The guard motions with his gun for Tim to move out. The roof is low, Tim has to stoop. He takes a step. The guard backs out of the doorway. The interaction seems absurdly civilised. Tim hurts all over. Stoop, he thinks is an old-fashioned word, no-one stoops any more, they slouch. Tim fixes the guard in his sight before ducking through the small doorway and stepping out into day.

Air, fresh with the smell of growing things, fills his lungs. He keeps his eyes on the guard. They are on different sides.

—Sides, teams.

The words repeat in his mind. Wind and sunlight frolic at the edges of his sight. Tim has a sense that he and the guard don't have to do this. His guard is small, his eyes empty. The others have vanished.

The guard signals for him to walk ahead.

Tim holds his ground; they could just go home.

The guard lifts his rifle, aims at Tim's chest without a

flicker of emotion and somewhere inside, Tim knows the guard would shoot him in exactly the same way; without emotion. He turns, taking in his cell, a man likes to see where he's been.

A small daub shack leans into the cliff face, hidden by the edges of the jungle. A store room for grain, for stock.

—For me.

Tim has a sense that he has fallen through a hole in the net. Fallen into another world, he shouldn't be here, he doesn't understand the rules. Numb, he follows a foot-beaten path into the jungle. The guard walks behind, his gun aimed at Tim's back. Tim can feel where the bullet will hit, there's a point between his shoulders.

—The bullet will sever the spine.

The knowledge is without emotion, Tim notes that.

His awareness is in his senses; his ears unravel the chaotic blur of sound to single threads, each bird pitched clean one over the other; his eyes liberate detail from mass, chlorophyll pulses through leaves at the touch of sunlight, dusted grasses are edged with razor teeth, poison sleeps in the squamous pulp of succulents; beyond the fresh of new growth is rot, decay is a whisper.

—Run!

—No!

His body jerks with the impulse.

—Run like an animal and you'll die like one.

His father is in his head.

Tim's heart races. He forces his body to walk, just walk. He doesn't want to be a fucking idiot.

—There'll be a right time.

—What if there's not?

—There will. Just don't panic.

Around the next bend the track ends. There is a small clearing. He's blown it. There's nowhere to go.

—Nowhere to run.

—Should've run.

The place holds a smell of rotting, insects buzz around his ears, seek out his eyes.

He feels the guard's gun at his back nudging him forward. He takes a small step like an old man's. His blood pumps through him with sickening sensation.

—Fuck this for a place to die!

He spins around. He'll fight. Kill the fucking guard. The guard is quick, steps back centred with his gun. Eye to eye with dead eyes, Tim's breath catches. His guard's a boy. Behind the dirty white lungi they are a boy's eyes.

The Boy gestures towards the clearing with his gun, says something Tim doesn't understand.

Tim just stands there staring like a dumb beast, staring at the child soldier with the dead eyes.

The Boy gestures again towards the clearing.

Numb, Tim turns and looks. This time he sees the bucket, sees the hole in the ground spewing forth life like Pandora's box. He begins to laugh.

—It's a shit hole.

His guard's a boy. And he's just faced death on the way to the dunny.

Laughter throws the Boy who raises his gun, spits a warning.

'OK! OK!'

Tim holds up his hands and backs into the clearing, he's bursting to piss.

The Boy lowers his gun.

Dubious, Tim peers into the bucket, half a plastic soft

drink bottle floats in water riddled with wrigglers. Water. His mouth makes its own, he'd give anything for a drink.

Flies seek out the dried blood on the side of his head, want to drink from the corners of his lips and eyes. He brushes them away, checks out the shit hole. It is a living thing. He couldn't squat and shit in it even if he wanted to, be too scared something would crawl up his bum. He can piss in it though.

The release is sweet. The moment almost normal. Except for having his wrists cuffed.

—Not really into that.

There's a jokester in his head.

Looking down, Tim notices his feet, big, solid on the ground. Tanned. He remembers Rimpoche pointing to his feet once and asking if they were him, Tim? He said, no, they were just his feet. It had been easy to dismiss his feet. Tim looks at his hands. He's always liked his hands. The first signs of real ageing are beginning to show in the grain of his skin. Suddenly he doesn't know what else he is besides these hands, these feet.

It had been easy to visualise offering up his limbs to the hungry ghosts with a full belly. To think himself wise, unattached. Now it isn't so easy. If he dies the hungry ghosts will still be hungry.

He doesn't want to die. Doesn't know what else he is besides this body, not really, not now.

The Boy orders him to hurry, get on with it.

Tim squats. Wets his hands. Bathes from the bucket, as best he can. Bathes the side of his head. Tries to soften the blood that flakes and pulls at the edges of the wound. His fingers tell him the gash is shallow. He breathes in sharply at his own touch, the pain is in his skull and in the welt. Tim wonders if it was the Boy who struck him.

Walking back, Tim scans the jungle looking for signs of the others. They wouldn't have left him alone with a boy.

—Or would they?

Maybe he should run. Might be his last chance. Tim's heart begins to race.

—Too easy?

—Easy! He's got a bloody gun.

—But he's a boy.

They round a bend in the path and the hairs on the back of Tim's neck stand, someone's there, to his left. He can feel them, he just can't see them. The jungle's camouflage is complete, at least to his eyes.

Tim stops at the door of the shack. He can't step through the doorway willingly. The whole situation is ridiculous. For the first time he understands that what you don't do has as much meaning as what you do. The realisation ripples in his heart, it's too big for the moment.

He turns, faces his guard. A protest.

The Boy is quick with a blow to Tim's kidneys.

Tim spits dirt from his mouth. Old energies rise. He is filled with the pride of a hard, dry land, his grandfather and his father.

A gun to his head, the Boy drags him to his feet to frogmarch him into the shack. Tim wants to punch the little bastard's lights out. Has to remind himself that boys with guns are dangerous. Easy to startle, quick to fire.

Tim ducks as he's shoved through the small doorway.

The Boy slams the door closed behind him. Bolts it. Shuts out the light, the air.

Tim's eyes take time to adjust, and in the half dark, the smells of the store room rise on the already building heat like souls from hell. Tim breathes through his mouth. This isn't the Asia he knows. The dirt floors he'd found so charming seem to him now like Disneyland copies. There's nothing charming about this floor, it stinks of poverty and a passionless desperation that only comes when you have nothing left to lose.

His eyes adjust. In the middle of the room there is a bowl and a cup. A drink!

It's hot. He draws in the liquid with short sharp breaths, unable to wait. It's tea, black and sweet. The pleasure's intense. When he pauses the cup is almost empty. He feels like a fool. He should have made it last, taken a few sips at a time.

When he was a boy his father used to take him orienteering. They'd go out into the desert for a couple of days at a time. Carry everything they needed. The Captain would have the map in his head, and Tim would be the eyes. He hated those trips. They never carried enough water. The Captain prided himself on making a little last, wanted Tim to be able to do the same.

Tim sits, puts the cup beside him on the floor. Picks up the bowl and sniffs, rice slop. He wonders if the rat's been at it. Pokes at it with a finger. His stomach rumbles. He doesn't know how long it is since he last ate. It was before he got on the bus. Twelve hours? Two days? He doesn't know.

The thought of the rat at his food really puts him off, but he's fucking hungry, and disease suddenly seems a bit of a long-term concern. He rounds the rice into a small ball between the fingers of one hand. It's awkward getting the rice to his mouth with cuffed wrist.

—Sometimes people don't have choices.

The rice has stones. Tim chews slowly, grinds the thought with his teeth.

—Choice.

How the fuck did he get involved in this?

—If I'd caught the morning bus.

—But I didn't.

He meant to. But then she smiled, said shyly, she was going to the market. Asked if he would like to come. And he stayed.

—Sweet.

Is how he saw her.

—Different. Pretty. Thai.

—How a girl should be.

Tim smiles at his own simplicity. He has no idea what she was really like. That's just how he saw her. Western women shoved their balls in your face. Eastern women had the courtesy to hide them. It made the interaction easier. For him at least.

Fate in retrospect is always choice. If it had been Vera, he'd have gone. He pushes a stone out of his mouth with his tongue, feels his humanness in the warmth of his breath and the moisture of his lips. On the edges of his consciousness is a sense of his life, fine filaments, fragile, unconnected.

He hears voices. Freezes. His hands pause above the bowl. The voices recede and then are gone. Tim begins to chew again. Pushes the food slowly around his mouth. He wonders when they'll come. What will happen next. He has never really appreciated the sweetness of rice before.

Finished, he leans back against the wall, his cup beside him. Sweat beads on his forehead. His cell is a sweat box, the heat suffocating. Visions of Paul Newman dragged, defiant, from his hellhole in *Cool Hand Luke*, play across Tim's mind.

—I am breathing in, I am breathing out, I am breathing in.

But this is the part they didn't show in the movie and Tim's thoughts play havoc with him.

—Perhaps the voices weren't soldiers.

He doesn't think he heard the Boy's voice. He's sure he didn't.

—Should have called out.

—That's what I should have done, called out.

And it occurs to Tim it could be months before anyone notices he's missing. His body reacts. His lungs contract, make it hard to breathe.

'Oh fuck.'

He doesn't like this.

—Except Mischa.

Tim breathes out long and slow. When he was a child and got asthma his mother made him blow into a paper bag.

'Yeah, Mischa'll notice.'

The thought expands. He doesn't want Mischa to notice.

—He'll think the wrong thing.

Tim imagines Vera sitting on the end of Mischa's bed.

'You know what your Dad's like, hon. He's probably forgotten what month it is. He's always late. Probably even be late for his own funeral.'

Tim knows Mischa will smile then, when she says that, he always does. Tim's mind spins off into thoughts of Vera.

—She's good with words.

—What she says always sounds right.

—But it's not always.

—Not all of it.

Anger sours the rice in his belly. Vera doesn't know how much work it takes to keep distant. He'd like to think of himself as 'a rolling stone', but the image in his mind is of a pebble. Lonely is a place he doesn't go.

He stands, to shake it off. Hits his head on a beam of bamboo.

'Fuck you too! Fuck you all!'

He kicks the wall. It's rock, it hurts.

'OK, OK.'

Tim's quick to rein himself in. Pull himself together. Kicking's not going to help. He's got to think. Use his head. Why have they taken him?

—Because they think I'm someone else.

—But they've got my passport.

—Have they?

—They must have.

Tim hasn't even thought about his money belt, his bags. They'd know a lot about him from his bags; his petcha, the pictures of Mischa, his passport. It dawns on Tim that who he is, is not important, it's what he is. White, foreign.

Sweat runs down the back of his legs. It's too hot. He can't think properly, can't breathe. He sits again. His mind fills with the image of a pencil-drawn map of northern Thailand, her borders; there are two points marked in red, his father and himself; his father loses his sight and he will die; the moments are separated only by time.

—Vera'd call it a curse.

Without warning the bolt is drawn. Tim's caught off guard. Anger knots the muscles in his back, his lip curls, he stares at the two men standing in the doorway, big with their guns and their faces covered.

Get up! The command is without words.

Tim wipes anger from his mouth with the back of his hand and stands.

Outside, with their rifles levelled at his chest, Tim faces his captors without fear.

'English?' he asks, looking at the soldier he thinks of as the Captain because he reminds him of his father. For Tim the similarity is not just the way they stand.

'Do you speak English?'

The Boy steps in, shoves Tim in the back. Without thinking Tim shrugs him off. And in the brief pause between action and reaction, steps towards the Captain.

'Tim,' he says, hands over heart.

The Boy is quick with his gun to the back of Tim's head. The gun wins. Tim backs off.

—A good little prisoner.

The Boy leads them through the jungle. Through the confusion of tangled vine, shadow and reflected light, without hesitation. Tim can't even work out which direction they're heading. He can't see the sun. Only pinpricks of blue shining through a canopy of green. At home he always knows where he is. Here it is the Boy who knows where he is.

The memory of white-blue fills Tim. The unending summer skies of his childhood. The path of the sun clear in the open scape, that wraps itself around the edge of the world. Longing washes through Tim, with the remembered smell of rain on hot dry grass. His mind makes a painting. A line of ochre, a line of sun-bleached blond, a thin horizon. Two lines against a vast expanse of sky. Tim hasn't painted for a long time.

The heat and the rhythm of walking stretch out his thoughts. Australia. The Ancient name for her dances on the edges of his mind. Gondwanaland. He lets the word in. No-one will know. Wonder land, large and resting. His body remembers the soft talc of her between his toes. He's white, but here it is, quietly hidden in him, the land and a need to go home.

Longing shapes Tim's anger, dreaming of home isn't going to get him there. As they walk Tim pays attention, tries to calculate their direction from the angle and refraction of the light and what he knows of the sun's path. Maths. There is a place beyond feeling in fact. In the translation of degree and angle into knowledge.

In the desert, his father had been able to feel direction in the slope of the land, the grain of the soil and the heat of the sun, more accurately than Tim had been able to guide them with his eyes.

—North-east!

As they head into the mountains Tim thinks perhaps they are heading north-east.

Walking hurts. The ground is uneven and with his hands tied, Tim's shoulders and neck spasm, sending shooting pains into his skull. As much as Tim can't believe that this is happening, each step brings him closer to the feeling that all of this is familiar; the sweat, the heat, the pain. Part of him has always been expecting it to happen.

—Movies.

He tells himself.

—It's all the bloody wars we watch.

His head is filled with images of strong, silent, enduring men.

He trips, a dead branch trapping the sole of his sandal.

—Don't drag your feet!

His father's in his head again.

—Inadequate.

The word comes to him. He's always felt inadequate. He almost laughs. It's the timing of his realisation that appeals to him.

—Really going to help.

The sun draws moisture from foliage, fills the air with a damp weight that is suffocating. Tim stumbles. A drink becomes all he can think of. His eyes bore holes into the Boy's back, willing him to stop, take a break, take a drink. He doesn't. He shows no sign of tiring, his shirt pulls tight with each step across young muscles.

Tim stumbles again. Falls on hands and knees.

'Wait!' his voice cracks.

The Boy does not.

Tim is yanked to his feet. Has to try and catch his breath and still keep up. Fingers of sweat run from his hairline, tickle close to his ears, drive him crazy.

He's prodded in the back to get him moving; he's falling behind!

Tim turns on the soldier, jaw clenched.

'Fuck you!'

The soldier is laughing. It's in his eyes.

Tim's anger springs from the place childhood injustices are stored. He hasn't been there for years. Tim hates being made to do. Something inside him snaps. He used to run long distances. He turns and follows the Boy.

—Let them scramble to keep up.

On cold mornings his father would make him strip off, down to his shorts, and run, and keep on running. Tim hated it. Until one day, hating, he pushed himself to run even faster. Pushed himself beyond the point of his reckoned endurance, willing the valves in his heart to burst, so that his father would learn. But the valves in his heart didn't burst. Instead, he found a place beyond the ache of muscles, where the heart releases and stops fighting.

Gaining on the Boy, Tim pushes himself harder, picks up the pace. The pounding in his head becomes a concentrated tone.

Now Tim is on the Boy's heels and can smell him, dusted in spice.

The Boy shoots a look over his shoulder.

Tim smiles. Not with his eyes.

He's pushing the pace from behind. Rivers of sweat cut across his body, run down his legs. He can feel his own heart set to bursting.

—Soon, soon . . .

Suddenly the Boy turns on him, sends him flying. Tim rolls, he's past hurting. Eyes wide, he howls like a demon as the Boy comes for him. He's broken the little bastard. A boot connects with his rib.

The Boy is hauled off. Held by the Captain like a puppy by the scruff of the neck. Tim spits blood from his mouth. Laughs.

The Boy makes a grab for him. The Captain throws the Boy backwards roughly. Beats him around the head with quiet, brutal words and rough hands. Only then does Tim see what he's done. The Boy is a sapling, grown to that stage of long limb and easily offended heart. His anger's moist.

Tim closes his eyes and breathes in deep. He's no different from his father.

Tim is kicked to get up. Struggles to stand. He looks at the Boy.

—Sorry.

He wishes he knew how to say it.

Tim notices the soldier who laughed at him is not laughing now. The Captain holds out a canteen for Tim to take a drink. Tim leans forward. The Captain holds the canteen back, just a little. Just enough to make Tim reach. And reach again.

Tim gets the message. He doesn't like it but he gets it. Tim straightens. Looks the Captain in the eye. Surrenders.

The Captain smiles, crow's-feet underline his satisfaction.

He holds the canteen steady.

This is the language of men.

Mischa lifts a model Stealth F–1/17 above his head. Looks up at the flat broad underbelly. When he grows up he's going to be a pilot. There's a blob of glue, he wipes it off with the cuff of his windcheater. Runs his thumb along the edge of the wing. When he's a pilot he'll fly his Dad wherever he wants to go.

In the heat the jungle sweats.

They've been walking for hours. Tim plants his foot, grinds a small succulent into the ground, feels pleasure.

—Not like me.

Tim shivers.

—Today I'm not like me.

—Exhausted.

Is not just a thought. It's how he feels. Strung with exhaustion. Every muscle hurting, every bone. Even his skin hurts. He thinks his wrists are bleeding again but pain has become a constant static, so maybe they're not. The only thing he is certain of is the Boy's hatred. He is in the eye of a storm of his own making.

The jungle becomes steeper. Pushing upward, close together, Tim struggles. Leans into each step, concentrates on his footing. He doesn't want to fall, not here without hands. Soil crumbles under his feet, the smell of it rises strong to mix with his own scent.

—Locker rooms.

Exhausted, Tim's mind throws up images of other times, all rolling him towards this, here and now, and that's where logic shatters. Tim can't even be bothered to try and make sense of it any more. Step and breathe, he focuses there, lets his mind free fall.

'Which way?' His father wants to know.

He has blindfolded Tim, taken him to the bottom of the garden and now he wants Tim to find the house. In memory, Tim feels himself a weedy boy, step out tentative.

'Think before you move!'
His father's never pleased.

The image Tim holds most clearly of his father is that of a cold man, in a neatly pressed suit without any human wrinkle.

His mother saves him.

—'Tea time!'
She smiles as Tim rips off the blindfold and bolts up the backyard. She thinks they've been playing. Her boys playing.

Step and breathe.

They weren't playing. And it wasn't fun. Tim feels movement in his belly, a slow curling.

Step and breathe.
His stomach cramps. It's the twisting of hurt into hate, his feelings work his body because he won't name them. He concentrates on the ground.

Step and breathe. Step and breathe.
The cramp passes.

Looking up, Tim realises he's on level ground. They're on a ridge and there is sky heavy with grey and the promise of rain. But it won't come yet. The monsoon's not due yet. Another week at least. That was something he'd heard one man say.

—North!
Suddenly it's clear to Tim they're heading north. Even with the sky choked with cloud he can feel the sun sinking to his left. He almost laughs. He's worked it out.

He's pushed to sit, his back against the rock.

The soldiers squat, rifles across their knees. Smoke in silence. Even the Boy. Tim wouldn't mind a cigarette right now. No-one offers him one.

—M1, M16s. American.

Now Tim looks, he knows what their rifles are. He turns the knowledge over in his mind, as though it were the weapon.

The sound of a truck comes from the valley. Every hair on Tim's body stands straight. He listens hard. Tracks the familiar sound. The road runs north–south, he can make out the direction by following the sound. He never knew he could do that.

He looks up. He's being watched. 'Don't!' That's what Tim reads in the Captain's eyes.

—Or was that a film I saw?

Pain, lack of food, water, and exhaustion, bleed Tim's thoughts one into another. He has walked through the looking glass and there is too much green in the picture.

He licks his lips. He is offered water. He drinks, and with each cool mouthful he reasons.

—North is Burma.

The Salween River and the Burmese border. He looks for signs of a river. Listens for one. Can make out nothing. Still he knows they're heading north. And now he thinks about it, he knows there's been border trouble between Burmese refugees and some Buddhist freedom army.

—A Buddhist army, what a contradiction.

That's why he read the article.

—The Burmese Buddhist Student Front, that was it!

He remembers he didn't even have to read between the lines to work out the whole thing was a set-up. The Buddhist Student Front had links with the government. That's why they crossed the border and killed their own.

—So why would they take me?

—Australia has companies in Burma. Supports the government.

At least Tim thinks they do.

—Fucking fascist. Anything for money.

He looks at his guards, wonders if they've noticed his blessing cords.

If the soldiers are Buddhists it might make a difference if they know he is too. There are no trappings he recognises and he can tell nothing from their faces. A man's eyes may be the windows of his soul but they give little information about his political allegiance. Tim wonders for a minute what he expected. That they would embrace like brothers united in a common faith and everything would change.

He smiles at his own naivety. He's tired, very, very tired. He rests his eyes, shuts out the soldiers, the day.

—A Buddhist who kills is not a Buddhist at all.

Another truck passes.

—I kill ants.

—Yeah. But who can take an ant seriously?

As the sound of the truck fades into the distance, Tim registers there's been two trucks in five minutes.

—Two is a lot. Must be near the border!

His body dips into sleep. He doesn't know what he thinks about anything any more. He lets himself go.

Mosquitoes herald the coming of night. Circle Tim's ears.

He can see them. Big mosquitoes. Black smudges against a grey sky. He's dreaming.

—Mosquitoes in Amsterdam.

That had really surprised him. He's bitten. Scratches.

Separates from his dream. Opens his eyes. His mouth is dry. His neck's stiff. He's rusted.

—Old.

He thinks, and the places he's been and the things he's seen well up inside of him; fireflies in Nepal; mountains, stained through the rhythm of the tides, on sea shells; bare-chested horsemen who carry the old world in their saddle bags and drink chung out of hand-beaten silver cups; babies swimming like turtles.

Tim looks at the soldiers, squatting, waiting. Dusk lends itself to his sense of separation. He sees the soldiers as a painting. Hard edges softened and the quiet captured in the tone. He'd call it, 'Night Watch'.

It's time. The three soldiers stand as one, as though answering some call Tim has completely missed hearing. He notices their boots, army issue. He is dragged to his feet, gagged. He doesn't resist, he's sore and tired, and hasn't a clue how he fell into this underworld. He's a surface dweller, likes to keep things simple. He wonders what they want in exchange for his life.

—Equal rights and justice?

—What his life is worth?

—The release of a hundred political prisoners?

—Two hundred?

—The establishment of democracy?

—The preservation of culture?

Tim laughs at the thought. It's just his life. How could his life be worth so much?

—Life is cheap.

In Asia this is true. In Kosovo. In Africa. Tim's head spins. None of it makes sense.

The Captain leads them down into the shadow nightfall

of the jungle. The Boy rides Tim's tail. The thought of dying for the Boy's democracy definitely does not seem worth it to Tim. Shadows catch Tim's eye. The Boy starts.

—He's afraid.

Tim can feel it.

—If you go down to the woods today you're in for a big surprise.

The Boy's scared. Once Tim might have felt the same. Now he sees it as a weakness; stores the knowledge.

Tim doesn't like what's happening to him, the way he's beginning to think. If he just knew who they were, what they wanted, maybe he could find some logic for all of this. Some connection between his life and theirs, that would make sense of it, at least to him.

—Karma!

He thinks.

—Yeah, but who the fuck knows what that means?

It's not so simple.

—There's individual karma.

—Generational karma.

—Geographical karma.

—Historical karma.

It's not always easy to work out what lesson you're supposed to be learning.

The Boy shoves him in the back to get a move on. Tim slips. Digs the edges of his sandals into the side of the mountain to stop himself losing his footing. Grazes his hands on rock. Feels the hot spring of anger. Breathes deep and reminds himself that it has taken countless lifetimes to reach this point. All beings have at one stage been his mother. Even the Boy. And he must treat them all with loving kindness. Tim ignores the whispered interjection that he hasn't had much luck practising this with his own mother. But objectively he can do it.

—No problem.

The Boy urges him forward.

—But if he shoves me in the back again I'll kill him.

In the distance Tim thinks he sees lights. The ground gives way to a flatter gradient and the jungle begins to thin. The Captain stops. Tim hears another truck, it's rolling down into the valley, coming towards them. Soon he'll see the lights, know where the road is!

Without warning he's hooded, in a sack smelling of mildew and flour. He pulls back. Shakes his head. Tries to get the damn thing off. The Boy knocks his feet out from under him. Once he's down the Boy's boot strikes hard.

—Not the kidneys!

Tim rolls. Is hauled to his feet snorting like a bull. Inside the stinking weave of the sack he has to work for air. He's held tight. Made to stand still. The gun hooked under his ribs is good incentive. The truck passes, close.

Only when the truck drops through its gears and starts to pull out of the valley do the soldiers begin to edge forward, Tim sandwiched between them. In the distance dogs bark. Tim thinks he hears singing.

—A village!

They are moving towards the song, towards the village. Inside the sack sound offers Tim his only point of reference. The singing is close now. Tim is reined in to stop, pushed to stand his back flat against a wall; bamboo.

The song finishes in a burst of drunken laughter and shouted comment. If they'd just shut up Tim could make them hear him. They don't. Someone knocks quietly on a door. There is the drag of it opening and light. Bright through the weave of the sack. Tim is pulled forward.

Another song lurches towards a rhythm.

Tim shrugs off the guard's hands, throws himself backwards and screams. The sound is a howl. A gun is jammed hard into his gut. Cuts the sound. He is rolled through the doorway. Into a space smelling of sump oil and acetone.

He is thrown to sit and then apparently forgotten. Someone lights a cigarette and men talk in urgent whispers. Tim wonders what he should do. He hurts.

Without warning the sack is pulled from his head, his pupils dilate, his eyes snap shut. He's pulled to his feet and dragged to stand in front of a truck; a Mercedes 14/12, red. He's in a garage.

Tim notices one of the fuel tanks has been opened at one end, like a can of beans. The metal plate of its base rests against the front tyre, next to an arc welder. Slowly these images join together in Tim's mind like the pieces of a puzzle.

—No fucking way!

He backs off shaking his head.

—You're not going to bloody seal me in that thing!

Now he's prepared to fight.

The Boy grabs him from behind.

Tim throws him off.

The Captain grabs him by the hair, drags him towards the truck. Tim scrambles to keep up with his head, get his feet to take some of his weight. He's thrown down hard against the truck, his head crashing into the rear wheel.

He pulls back, his vision swims. The numbers of the hub meter go round and round; one, something,

something, six, six, four. He's hauled to his feet by the Captain. Made to look at the truck, as an old man, hands stained with grease, pulls a clear plastic tube from the fuel tank. Places it in his mouth and inhales. Grinning, he repeats the action.

Tim feels the blood drain from his face, betraying his understanding.

The old man laughs, nods. He has an almost toothless grin and the eyes of a sadist.

Caught in this moment, like a bear in a trap, Tim knows there's nothing he can do. All the fight goes out of him.

The Captain releases his grip.

Moment falls into moment; there is a key; his handcuffs are taken off; he is given water. A cascade of images distils into single frames within Tim's mind; the guard's hand as he passes the canteen; the bare light bulb above him; the open fuel tank; the guards' faces, eyes only staring out at him, unreadable, from behind their cloth shrouds.

Mischa wakes in fright.

He's crying. His heart hurts. He can't remember his dream, he just has the feeling.

He's at the side of his Mum's bed, crawling in, before he even realises that's where he's going. She's warm. He's cold. She uncurls. Takes him in. Rubs his feet between hers. Joe stirs, gets up to piss, 'You OK mate?'

Mischa nods.

Joe nods, he's not awake.

Vera mutters something, her love is warm and gets caught in Mischa's hair. She strokes his head. Gentle. And snores.

Sleeved in the truck's fuel tank,

Tim breathes through the tube, tastes petrol fumes on his tongue. Someone shoves at his legs, forcing him in tighter. He takes up the smallest space possible.

—Slim Tim the size of a pin.

An old remembered taunt.

—Yeah well, I'm not so fucking slim now.

His shoulders wedge tight across the width of the tank. There is a scraping and banging and then the light is gone.

—They're sealing the tank.

The sound of the spark striking an arc sears Tim's nerves. He breaks into a sweat. Burned alive, buried alive, these are the images that fill him.

—I am breathing in. I am breathing out.

He fights them with his breath. Horror wins.

—I can't do this!

He kicks out. His feet strike the seal, someone yells. He kicks again. The next instant his feet are burning. He screams. Losing the tube from his lips, his lungs fill with the stench of his burning soles and flux. Desperate, he gasps for the tube, his teeth clench it tight, he breathes and breathes.

He hears water, they're cooling the tank. The crack of the arc strikes again. He closes his eyes. Concentrates on the tube between his lips, nothing else, and breathes. Again the crack of the arc is followed by the sound of water.

Locking down behind closed eyelids, sound and sensation mix in Tim's mind, with remembered sharp colour images from articles in *Time* and *Newsweek*, exposing the truth about the Palestinian, Vietnamese, Rwandan, Serbian crises. Image overlays image. Tim's mind races.

—There are always pictures.
—Pictures of victims.
—People caught in the mess.
—Like me.
—There'll be pictures of me.
—But not of this. They'll never know.

It seems such a silly thought but Tim's never understood before that by the time there are pictures the worst of it is over, people are already dead.

He breathes in through the tube, out through his nose. Sounds and voices blur, everything seems cottoned with fluff. His mind says flux.

—I'm breathing too deep.
—No. No I'm not breathing enough. Not getting enough.

The truck rocks, someone is stepping into the cabin. Tim imagines it's the Captain; heavy boots on a rusted, once red step.

—It could be the Boy.

But Tim can't imagine the Boy's hand on the pitted steering wheel as he reaches over to start her up. He can only imagine a man's hand.

The truck shudders, old lungs after a bad night, the engine turns over.

—Ignition!
—We have lift-off Houston.

In Tim's head the clowns have come out to play. He laughs. His tears are cool on his hot face. He didn't know he was crying. He feels himself a boy, breakable. But as a boy he hadn't been breakable. Even when his father locked him in the cupboard under the stairs he didn't cry. It's only now, as a man, he makes such a weak boy.

Cocooned in the rough idling of the truck, Tim registers here and now only in changes of texture; a wooden bridge; a steep descent; the changing camber of the road, from dirt to the even hum of bitumen, beyond that, real is questionable.

The remembered smells of butter, tea and incense come to him. In his mind he's walking up the rough stone stairs of Rimpoche's Gompa. Passing walls of maroon and gold, dirty from the grubby hands of little monks. There is the sound of cymbals and chanting as he passes the second level. The smell of ucha and palak as he passes the third. And the excited scamper of Rimpoche's snow lion dogs as he breaks onto the fourth, their too long dew-claws tapping across the marble mandala floor.

—How many times have I walked those stairs?

Tim breathes in long and slow through the tube, remembers the shining, polished faces of his sanga, the inner circle of Western disciples, when they'd gather outside Rimpoche's rooms for special teachings. None of them ever looked the same when he saw them on the street.

An image comes to Tim of hardened faces and fingers too busy counting mantras to scramble in pockets for loose change. In the East local Westerners look right through beggars.

—It's not right.

—It's how it is.

Tim's mind is filled with contradiction. His mother always told him, 'Let he who has not sinned cast the first stone'. He's sinned. He's walked right past beggars. He plays with the tube between his teeth.

—Suffering. There are three kinds of suffering.

He remembers the teaching.

—The suffering of being human; old age, sickness and

death. The suffering of suffering; the personality, the mind. And the suffering of change.

—Vera changed things.

The words are felt more than thought. He really does remember the teaching on suffering, and remembering, he sees differently than he did at the time.

They are all there, his sanga, and Vera. It is her first trip to Nepal, the first time he's let her step into his world. Rimpoche is speaking. Truth unfolds without effort. But Tim's truth is in his body, in the tension he carries in his chest.

Beside him Vera keeps nodding, agreeing with everything Rimpoche says, she looks like one of those stupid dogs on the back dash of old Holdens.

—She embarrassed me. Changed everything.

—Before Vera it was easy.

Before Vera Tim remembers feeling worthy, being able to listen to teachings undistracted, a good student. Remembers Rimpoche's laughing face and the feeling when his teacher would clap his hands and say, 'Ar! Very good question Tim!' Remembers the feeling of pride.

That day he had no questions. Vera irritated him, distracted him, exposed him.

—Petty—Flawed—Normal.

—Rimpoche was my hero.

Tim could weep. Vera was good at normal. She made things small and put them on sandwiches. And he hated her for that.

The thought of sandwiches always makes Tim think of his mother. Grinding down through its gears the truck slows. Tim's skull and neck take the pressure. His spine will snap just below the skull. He fills his lungs. Makes himself fill the space. Holds his body tight to take the weight of his own mass, relieve the pressure on his head and spine.

The truck lurches to a stop. Edges forward and stops again.

Tim is back in his body, present, alert. The sound of engines fills the darkness like a cacophony of crickets.

—A road block. The border!

—What happened to the river?

Tim's mind races.

—Maybe we already crossed the river.

—Maybe they drugged me.

—Maybe this is my last chance.

He fills his lungs. Breathing in deep he tastes heavy metals on his tongue. He holds the tube tight between his teeth. Yells as loud as he can. Kicks the side of the tank. Draws in more air. His head spins. The edge of sound blurs, and his muscles relax, chemical sweetness.

He forgets to listen, yawns. In his mind the road block has become a traffic jam. He's comfortable, everything's stopped hurting. He can think of worse ways to die.

The truck rocks, the driver's stepping down. At the back of Tim's mind he knows this but the thought keeps slipping. Through the carbon monoxide blur comes the sound of knocking, the banging of drums . . .

—A checkpoint. It's a checkpoint!

Tim remembers. Kicks the side of the fuel tank, a blunt sound that gets lost in the night's confusion, the sound of engines idling and rough men's dealings.

The truck rocks again, the driver's climbing in. Tim kicks, screams, 'Here! I'm here! In HERE!'

The truck pulls away into the cool freshness of the open road, Tim breathes it in, the sound of his own voice trapped in the tank with him. The moment lost, Tim is suddenly unbearably tired. He's had enough. He just wants to sleep, to forget. He lets go, if he breathes he will do it without thought. Down, down, wham! There's oxygen in the fresher air of the road. He's flung back into consciousness.

The truck veers off the main road, bounces over potholes.

—Jesus!

He aches. The side of his head throbs. His bones push hard into his joints. He's confined, crammed into himself. He feels sick from the carbon monoxide. The truck drops down through the gears with the weight of ascent.

—Out.

—I've got to get out.

—I can't breathe.

—Can't get enough air.

His lungs have seized. He could lose it now and when they arrive and cut him, like a sardine from his can, they'd find him dead.

—Fuck them!

—'Rage against the dying of the light.'

—It'd be too easy.

He's thinking clearly now, realises his jaw has clamped down tight upon the tube, cut off his air. Using his teeth, he bites it into shape, makes it round again. Breathe, he tells himself, breathe.

—And rage against the closing in of night.

At the back of Tim's mind is Vera; Mischa asleep on her lap.

—'Maybe each life has a measure of happiness and suffering. And it just sort of depends when it falls.'

Tim can hear her saying it. See her stroking their son's head.

—And this is my bit of suffering!

He snaps the thought, as though he were standing there in

front of her. Freaks himself out. His mind's playing tricks with him.

He opens his eyes. There's only black. Stinging black. He closes them again. Concentrates on breathing, tries to sketch the image of the Buddha in his mind. Let everything else go. But the outline is rough and ungainly, and everything else is clear. The image of Rimpoche's laughing face.

'Life is suffering Tim.'

And his father.

'What did you want? A dispensation?'

His father is laughing at him but it's not with kindness. A line of bitterness is etched in his blind eyes.

—A dispensation?

Tim thought he had one; he almost laughs.

—Should have been a comedian.

The truck shudders over loose wooden planks. His mind latches onto the sound.

—One-two-three-four-five-

—A bridge!

—Five planks.

—Not very wide.

—No. Only five planks.

The number repeats in Tim's mind. He adds it to the numbers of the hub meter.

—No. That's wrong. The numbers should go side by side.

—They're two separate pieces of information.

—Six hundred and sixty-four kilometres and a five-planked bridge.

Tim finds comfort in the fact of numbers.

—Fuck!

He hadn't thought. If he can see the hub meter again he

can work out how far they've brought him. How far he's got to get back.

There's a white-edged pain in his dick. He's got to piss. His kidneys ache, his waste is backed up all the way from his bladder. It's alright though because he can imagine the road now, because of the bridge with five planks, and he can see himself, walking back across it.

The truck nosedives into water, fast flowing, Tim feels it through the skin of the tank, cold.

—A ford. Not a fiord.

—We ford the river.

Memories from school.

Tim is pissing. The first he knows of it is the hot between his legs. There is no smell, he is breathing through his mouth, so it doesn't matter.

—Real suffering slices through the trunk of humiliation.

Tim doesn't usually think in poetic phrase. He likes it. Usually he thinks in pictures and doesn't draw conclusions.

—Not that I've been doing much of that lately. Drawing.

—Not until I got it into my head to draw mountains in the monsoon. To lose myself in grey.

—And look where that got me!

—No; wait!

—That wasn't the reason.

—I came for the monks!

—Didn't I?

Tim's heart begins to palpitate. Panic threatens to seize the workings of his lungs.

—I'm not myself.

—I'm poisoned.

—That's what it is.

—They've poisoned me.

Tim's whole system is poisoned. The truck shudders over another bridge.

—Bridge, creek, bridge.

He repeats the order of the crossings in his mind. He doesn't want to forget. What if he gets lost on the way back.

—What if I get lost?

Images from fairytales steal away his consciousness.

—Hansel and Gretel got lost.

Tim is gone, he doesn't care any more, his body will breathe as it will; or not.

A sense of space is the first Tim knows of the camp where he is to be kept. When they pull him from the tank his body is rock, and he is somewhere petrified inside. His jaw clamped around the air hose.

He is aware they are laying his body on the ground. Is aware there is light, soft like yellow butter. But he is somewhere else, arching backward, cool. His body filling a line of ancient grain. A splinter of wood, once soft, now rock. His mother's fossil of petrified oak. She keeps it on the mantelpiece and he's been dreaming there. He can see that now.

He tries to get up. A dying animal always walks its body out. He feels himself fall. Sees dust rise as his body hits the ground.

—A circle of fire.

—A ring around the moon.

—Maybe it'll rain.

A wave of nausea pushes itself through the poisoned cave of Tim's empty belly. Hot and cold dance like spring breezes through his blood. Perhaps he is sick on the floor.

Cool fingers on the back of his neck. Beautiful. And then something bitter on his tongue. Tim's body spasms. The light touch of fingers becomes hands, kneading the muscles on either side of his spine. He is bread. Rough unhulled grain and water, and she is forming him. Kneading him into shape. She works the muscles of his buttocks, his joints release, his legs straighten.

'Oh fuck!'

Pain punctures the chemical membrane that encases Tim's consciousness. His eyes begin to focus. Fractured images half lit; a woman's feet in the dust; red, the hem of her dress; truck wheels thick with mud.

—The hub meter!

Tim lifts his body. Tries to crawl. His vision swims. He hangs his head, breathes. There are hands in the dust in front of him. Dirty, stained to print like an etching plate. They are his hands.

Hate is a force. He stands. Reaches for the truck for support. His hand slips, he falls but doesn't hit the ground. The Captain has him by the back of the shirt. He pulls away, lurches forward, desperate. He wants to see the numbers on the hub meter.

Falling to his knees, a man of prayer, his hand slides across the hub of the rear wheel wiping away the mud.

—Seven hundred and twenty-three!

The numbers dance. He's hauled to his feet.

—Seven hundred and twenty-three.

All Tim can think about is the three rolling up with measured precision, caught halfway. He did it, he fooled them, he knows the numbers.

The Captain prods and pokes him. Examines him like cargo. He's sick of being handled. Looks for the woman.

She's gone. Or did he dream her? Tim's not sure. He wants to spit in the Captain's eye.

—Only a fool provokes confrontation when he cannot win.

—Ah Grasshopper.

As a teenager Tim loved that show. He hangs his head and locks his mind around the numbers.

—Six hundred and sixty-four from seven hundred and twenty-three.

His whole body's shaking. He's given water.

—Three from four is . . .

He drinks without thinking.

—No. Four from three.

—Four from three I cannot take . . .

Tim repeats the litany in his head.

—Fifty-nine!

The knowledge comes with a rush; he's travelled fifty-nine miles in that fucking fuel tank.

—Fifty-nine!

He looks into the empty cup, drops of water unboiled hold to its sides. He's always been so careful of what he drank in Asia.

—I didn't even think.

—Thirst, that's what they've done to me.

He hands the cup back. Someone grabs his arms. The Boy locks his wrists in chains, old, heavy. The Captain hands the Boy the sack. Time pauses for Tim in the crooked weft and warp of its weave. He puts it on in his own time. Slips it over his head as though he had a choice.

Outside the air is fresh, even through the mildew of the sack Tim tastes its sweetness on his tongue. He slides his feet. Doesn't want to fall. He's had enough surprises. The Boy shoves him forward, guides him with a hand on his shoulder and a gun to his back.

Tim hears voices, somewhere to his right. Drunken men, the rhythm of companions. In the distance a dog barks. Closer, another answers and is kicked. Tim catches the scent of roasting meat. His mouth waters for a barbecue.

Reality is out of sync. He is imagining square slices of bread, sausages and tomato sauce. He smiles. Private in the world of his flour sack.

Tim is bundled through a doorway into a room or hall. He is made to stand, his back against the wall. Always his back against a wall. Beneath the hem of the sack he sees the tops of his feet. The floor is wood. The Boy is a shadow guard Tim can barely make out through the weave of the sack. A smudge.

Tim feels himself drawing this moment. He knows the texture of the paper he would use and the silk of the soft grey lead. Someone passes silently in front of him. The Boy takes hold of Tim roughly by the shoulders. Directs him to the back of the house. To a room. Where the sack is pulled from his head.

The room is small. A cell. The Captain stands in the doorway. Fills it. Behind him is the Boy, gun slung across his chest. Tim keeps his eyes on the Captain. The Captain is enjoying the game.

'Eat,' he finally says and leaves.

The Boy closes and bolts the door.

Eat. The English word hangs in the air. Footsteps recede down the corridor. The Captain carries his weight in the heel of his step. The Boy's footfall is lighter. The sound of their boots carries through the bamboo of the house. The outer door is slammed and bolted shut. Then there is silence.

It takes Tim some seconds to accept he is alone. To feel free to breathe, to move, to look around. He takes in the small open window above the door. Its bamboo bars, and the light leaking from the hallway. He releases his breath. He hadn't realised he'd been holding it.

The room is only about seven foot by three. Its high bamboo walls are solid, open at the top for air, but barred. There is a sleeping mat, an old blanket, a bowl of food, a cup of water, and a bucket. The space feels hollow. Smells green. It's the bamboo. Cool fingers trace a path down Tim's spine. The night's little breezes. He shivers.

Someone laughs. A rough voice throws an insult. Tim sits on the edge of the sleeping mat. A stranger in another man's office.

After all these years,

Captain Rhyder still dreams in pictures. He's in the jungle. It's night. There's a trip-wire. He steps, cautious.

The phone rings.

In his dream the phone is an alarm. He's caught, sprung by the incessant ringing. Floodlights sweep the jungle. People run.

Captain Rhyder wakes reaching for the phone. A moment suspended in darkness. He barks down the line. Waking is never good. The even voice on the other end introduces itself.

'Bob Sutton, Consular Duty Officer with the Ministry of Foreign Affairs . . .'

Captain Rhyder throws the covers back. He needs his feet on the ground.

Bob apologises for phoning at such a late hour, ensures that he is speaking with Mr Rhyder. Father of Timothy James Rhyder. The Captain's back stiffens.

'Yes,' he says. 'Tim's my son.'

The even voice of Bob falters then.

'We arr . . .'

The Captain hears him draw breath before he continues.

'. . . The Ministry of Foreign Affairs that is, has been contacted by our Embassy in Thailand . . .'

The Captain's mind leaps ahead of Bob. Drugs he thinks. His son's been arrested.

—The stupid, fucking little . . .

His wife stirs. He hears the bedside lamp go on. He contains his anger in the set of his jaw, grounds himself in the contact of his ear against the receiver.

'Have you talked with your son recently, Mr Rhyder?'

'No,' says the Captain, 'not for months.'

His tone is curt. He's not going to lie for the little bastard.

'John?'

His wife wants to know who's on the phone.

He waves her quiet, stands. Wants Bob to get to the point, spit it out.

The point however is not what he's expecting. His son a hostage? It doesn't make sense. He feels nothing. Too blond, is all he can think.

Until suddenly thoughts and images, like too many people talking at once, crowd him.

—Not suited.

—Just a boy.

—No match for them.

—Not trained.

—Bamboo can kill.

—He should have been trained.

—He wouldn't be trained.

—I should have trained him. Made him!

Asia frightened Captain Rhyder.

'John?' His wife's voice is soft with worry. 'John?!'

It's the constant meter of the Consular Duty Officer, Bob Sutton's voice, that reaches the Captain. Leads him to the conclusion of their conversation with some sense of order.

'I think we should meet tomorrow at my office at ten o'clock. Hopefully by then we'll know more. And I'll be able to answer some of your questions.'

'Questions. Yes.'

Clearly there are questions to be asked. The Captain is grateful Bob is good at his job.

'Thank you,' he says, 'Thank you for letting us know.'

He hangs up the phone.

'John what is it?'

There's too much breath in his wife's question.

'John! Please tell me!'

She's rarely this insistent. He doesn't want to tell her, doesn't want a scene. He has an overwhelming desire for a cigarette. A walk to the Seven Eleven in the middle of the night and a cigarette. He hasn't smoked for fifteen years.

'John!' She puts her hand on his arm. 'What's happened? It's the middle of the night. Who was it . . .?'

He looks at her with his blind eyes.

She falls quiet.

It's cruel, he knows, but it satisfies him that his gaze shuts her up. Still he can't not tell her.

'It's Tim. They think he's been taken as a hostage.'

'Tim?' She almost laughs. It's the shock.

The Captain nods.

'He can't have been.'

The Captain sees red in the flash of a grenade.

'Can't have been! Why not? Because you don't want it that way!'

He pushes past her, reaches for his pants always neat on the chair opposite the bed. He can feel the blood pumping down his arms. That's why she stayed.

He can imagine the scene.

'Your husband's lost his sight Mrs Rhyder.'

'No. He can't have.'

But he had and Tim was, and the Captain still has the smell of the monsoon in him. Still hates rain.

—'Eat.'

Tim manages two mouthfuls of rice before his stomach cramps. He pulls his knees up to his chest and rolls onto his side.

—Not now.

—Not now.

He's far too tired. He closes his eyes, shuts out the world, and drops like a stone through water, into sleep.

Fever dreams play across his mind. He is the Boy, the older guard is his father. Is the Boy's father.

Men are laughing at him. His father and other soldiers. Their laughter hurts. He means to tell them to stop. But he can't move. They kick a dog. The dog is him. His grandmother picks him up out of the mud. The men's laughter rolls across the rice fields towards them.

Storm coming. His grandmother bows her head against the rain, as the wind wraps him in its roar and steals him from her arms. His grandmother turns screaming into the wind. His grandmother is Vera. But Vera is his mother; the shadow, watching from the kitchen.

His father is in the den. But the den is a bar. A soldiers' bar, in Asia. His father has the smell of napalm about him.

'It's his mother's fault. He's been too long in the company of women.'

All the soldiers laugh. His father licks his lips. His thoughts moist.

'I'm not sure he knows the company they're meant for.'

Dirty laughter swells the crotches of the soldiers. The shutters blow open.

'It's the lips between their legs you're supposed to be interested in, boy. Not their mouths.'

'Unless they're on their knees!'

The Captain's laughter is a force that backs Tim into another kind of life. A purer one than his father's where the perception is finer. And there she is. Tim can't see her face. He's caught in the beauty of sensation. Her veiled form delicate and rousing. The gentle strength of her legs. The fragrance of her skin.

Light falls on the rich textured pattern of cushions. The colours are bright. Tim wants her now. Wants her solid on the ground. He grabs for her. Pulls her to him. Rimpoche laughs. She has the smell of blood about her, strong like the earth. And it is in him. And he is rutting hard. Hard. And it is dark. And he can smell her.

'Ar,' he wakes. Or does he? His hand is wet on his belly. He is shining. He's never fucked like that. He licks his arm, needs salt. His stomach cramps. He needs to shit. No he doesn't. He's hot. He's very hot.

Consciousness slips from Tim like shifting shale beneath his feet.

At five in the morning,

the Boy sits silently eating rice, his gun beside him. He watches the old woman strain mint tea through a cloth. A moment before she turns to offer him the cup he looks away, as he has seen men do.

The old woman cooks for them. They took her from a Lahu village. All the younger women were sick and his Captain didn't want to eat food cooked from a sick hand. A sick girl might spit in his food, make him sick too, that's what he'd said. Lahu weren't Burmese, weren't loyal, they often sheltered the Shan.

The Captain took three boys from the village too, as porters. He shot them after they set up the camp in the deserted village. Told the old woman he'd sent them home.

The Boy used to be a porter, now he is a soldier, he picks up his tea. He was seven when he was taken from his village. Doesn't really remember his life before soldiers and guns. He knows his father died when he was very little and, that what you dream is important. His mother would ask him every morning. '*Ma-nay-nya ga bar dway ait-matt matt lae?*'

—Last night what did you dream?

Last night he dreamt about a black bear, very angry, with white teeth. His mother would tell him what the dreams meant. He doesn't know what they mean. But he knows he is from a Wa village. That he is Wa.

Tea finished, the Boy covers his face. Picks up his gun and heads towards the house where the prisoner is held.

Fed, dressed in boots, khaki pants, and an old shirt, the Boy tells himself he is well off.

Mist blankets the valley below. High in the jungle it has already cleared. The day will be hot.

The Boy pushes the cell door open with his foot, bathing the prisoner in weak light from the corridor. Tim opens his eyes.

'*Hey! htaung-thar dway, hta-hta.*'

The Boy is telling him to get up.

Tim closes his eyes. He's too sick.

The Boy enters. Prods him with his rifle. '*Taung/dar/dway.*'

Tim pulls away, curls into the wall. All he wants is for the Boy to go away. Leave him alone.

The Boy stands over him. Tim feels the threat of the Boy's boot close to his head. He doesn't care. He's too sick.

The Boy prods him again.

—Always at me.

Is a thought.

Tim's gut spasms. The pain forces him to open his eyes. Anything to get away from the pain, to distract him from the agony of his twisting bowel. His eyes burn hot. He feels the heat of them against the cool of air. The proportions of the cell have changed. Pain creates its own reality.

The Boy stares down at him. Tim imagines his mouth hanging open beneath his dirty turban. Dumb, is the word that comes to his mind, and he lets it in. He's past being careful. The word exposes him. Arrogant is not how he likes to see himself. But it's the truth.

Turning away, he tells himself he's just sick.

—That's all it is.

—I'm just sick.

Tim registers the Boy leaving. Pulls into himself. Sleeping is OK. Painless.

The sound of the cell door opening rouses Tim. He sees the Boy and the Captain.

—Like father, like son.

Tim tries to stand. It's what you do when an officer enters the room.

—An officer and a gentleman.

Tim laughs once. He's confused. His dreams are leaking into his waking. His stomach rises to meet the pounding in his head. He can't stand. He falls back against the wall.

The Boy and the Captain step aside, an old woman enters. She is small, bent. She takes Tim's hand. Feels for his pulse. Tim tries to hold the detail of her face in focus. She won't look at him. Keeps her eyes hooded. She is listening with her fingers. Tim's stomach cramps again. She feels his belly. Her fingers work his knotted bowel. The cramp passes. She's the one that helped him when he was pulled from the fuel tank. His body remembers her touch.

Recognition makes him smile. A cold sweat breaks out on his forehead, the precursor to a wave of nausea. He's going to be sick again.

'Oh fuck.' The words escape on his breath.

She covers his face with her small, cool hands.

—Cool is good.

Pins his eyelids shut with the pads of her thumbs.

—Gentle, so gentle.

Her touch belies the strength of her hands. She works her fingers beneath his hair, explores the planes of his skull.

When she is finished, she presses her palm to his forehead. Tim feels himself lean into her.

In the half light watching the small bent woman mix and grind herbs the three men are still. She grinds their politics in her pestle, arcs time. Extends the interval between moments of conflict long enough for Tim to exhale their differences and taste for an instant something else.

When she hands Tim herbs, in a cup mixed with water, he drinks without hesitation. At the first sweet touch of opiate his eyes close. Soon he is floating and only vaguely aware that he always has liked drugs.

His guards and the woman leave. To Tim their departure is a musical phrase; the percussion of locking enclosing, to the count of sixteen, the sound of receding footsteps. In his mind the musical phrase becomes a picture, abstract, charcoal on white.

The mark of his cell door, a squat vertical line, charcoal. The vibration of its locking bleeding into a thin horizontal line of smudged charcoal, contained between two lines of a drafter's pen. The charcoal is the footsteps, human, imperfect. The drafter's pen defines the corridor. Both end squarely in the final locking, a squat vertical, the reverse of the first, and the ending of the phrase.

The Captain stirs his tea.

Politically complicated, that's what Bob Sutton said about his son's abduction before he was called away unexpectedly and his assistant brought them tea.

The Captain thinks about the little he knows. That

Tim was taken from a bus in Thailand, apparently by Burmese rebels, many of whom are housed in refugee camps along the Thai–Burmese border. The Thai government is outraged. Has already placed curfews on the camps. Bob said there was some indication that the Burmese Buddhist Student Front may be responsible, although that was only speculation.

The Captain knows the Burmese Buddhist Student Front has links with the military junta. That information even made it to the newspapers.

—Yes, the situation is politically complicated.

No-one will want to make the wrong move, step on the wrong toes, diplomatically.

—All men can see the tactics whereby I conquer, but none can see the strategy out of which victory evolves.

The ancient saying of Sun Tzu's comes to the Captain's mind.

For more than thirty years he's drilled Sun Tzu's sayings, along with the study of South-east Asian politics into his students' minds. Tried to make them understand all warfare is based on deception. The Captain had not been prepared for the grenade that took his sight. The patrol was routine. Within safe territory. He learnt the hard way.

'Maybe we'll know more when Bob comes back?' his wife's words are a question, not a statement.

'Maybe,' he says.

And he wonders if Tim's even alive.

He sips his tea. The thick china cup familiar in his hand, a remnant of the days of the cafeteria. For the first time the Captain feels all sixty-one of his years.

'No-one drinks tea any more,' he says.

'No. Everyone drinks coffee now,' says his wife and forces a little laugh.

'Except us.' He smiles. He knows she drinks coffee when she's out, not with him. They fall back into silence. They've been assured; everything that can be done, will be done.

Tim wakes with a start.

Hits out at the air. There's no-one there. He's alone. He sits. Feels the too fast beating of his heart. It is day and the cell has lost its shadows. His eyes are drawn to the bamboo bars, where the daylight comes in. Daylight but little air. The cell is a sweat box. Outside the sun, a fire-breathing beast, consumes the air. He's got to piss. Stands to use the bucket.

The action forces him into his body. His mind begins to clear; the sun is not a beast. It's just suffocatingly hot. The cell walls are uncured and sweating. The last days come back to him; being bound, tied; the forced march; the fuel tank. His anger grows with the smell of his own urine, stronger and stronger. He doesn't even know if it's hours or days he's slept.

—This isn't my life.

There's tea in the cup. He drains it.

The cell door opens. The Boy stares at him standing, cup in hand.

'Hmm!'

The Boy is satisfied Tim is no longer about to die. He signals that Tim should pick up the bucket and come. The Boy will take him to wash. Tim is stopped at the cell door. A guard he's never seen before hands him the sack.

Tim is led from the cell with the sack over his head and the Boy's gun at his back. Outside he is directed to move along a narrow path. Shoved and prodded. Anger edges his reality. He slides his feet. The soil becomes damp, soft. He's reined in to stop. Made to kneel. Only then is the sack pulled from his head. They are on the edge of a river surrounded by jungle.

The moment distils for Tim into colour and light. He washes slowly. Too slowly for the Boy. Who kicks the bucket over.

'Fuck you.'

Tim buries the words under his breath.

—Bubbles from a drowning man.

Image sets itself against image. The bucket, the dirt beneath his fingernails. He hates the Boy.

Walking back to the cell, the sack damp and stinking over his head, Tim's mind rages that he is caught in this; someone else's hell. Vera always says nuns go to heaven because they believe in heaven. Personally he thinks they go to hell.

And war is his father's fault.

Again Tim refuses to enter the cell. The Boy is quick with a blow to his kidneys. Tim gasps. Is manhandled into his cell and the piss bucket thrown in after him. He rips the sack from his head, hurls it at the door. It falls like a feather.

The Boy draws the bolt.

Tim kicks the bucket, vents his frustration with his feet. The Boy walks away without a word.

'Fuck you. Fuck you all!' shouts Tim.

Anger is eating a hole in his gut. The Boy bolts the outer door. Alone, Tim gets a flash of himself, how he must look. Hunched, cradling hate in his belly like an animal.

'Not good. Not good at all,' he whispers.

—Our enemies are our greatest teachers.

Rimpoche's words come back to Tim. His teaching on compassion. Anger makes Tim clench his teeth. He wants to be able to yell in Rimpoche's face.

'Bet you didn't mean this sort of enemy!'

But he can't. Rimpoche had been talking about the Chinese. About this sort of enemy. Tim hadn't understood before.

For the first time in his life Tim feels really lost. All his doubt about his teacher, all his judgement of others comes now and stares him in the face. Nothing is as he thought it was. His mind shuts down.

There's fresh food in a bowl on the floor by the sleeping mat. His mouth waters. He sits. Takes a small amount of rice between his fingers. Everything changes, he tells himself.

—This'll end.

Tim is careful not to eat all the food at once. He must make it last. They only seem to feed him once a day.

—Hunger like anger must be tamed.

His head is filled with another man's words. He breathes in deep, feels his lungs expand to fill the cavity of his chest. Hollow, that's how he feels. He crosses his legs, closes his eyes, imagines breathing out the black and the fear.

'It'll be alright,' he whispers, and he lets his mind fall backwards into emptiness.

Crystal by coloured crystal he builds a visualisation. White light flows from the lotus heart of the Buddha into the crown of his head, washing away his human stink. Emptiness unfolds into a pure land, cradling him in its palm and the Buddha gazes down on Tim with loving eyes.

Comforted, he breathes deep and centres in himself. Only to notice the white light won't pass between his shoulder-blades.

—It never has.

Tim tries to dissolve the black between his shoulders. He can't.

—Fifteen years meditating and I'm still no fucking good at it.

His head begins to ache. He's working at resting in emptiness. Tim catches the contradiction; almost laughs.

The realisation that he is filled with theory eddies around him. He can hear himself define expressionism.

—The expression of that which is felt as opposed to an accurate pictorial rendering.

At twenty-two he got an A for art history and stopped painting.

—Buddha Nature.

Tim rocks as he recites the lesson.

'Is the source of all phenomena when free of the three conditions: being born, ceasing and remaining. Actual Buddhas are never born, because they abide in the unborn Dharmakaya; they never cease, because they are always in unceasing Sambhogakaya; and they never remain in limitation because they are always in never-remaining Nirmanakaya.'

He remembers the teaching word for word. But in the unnatural quiet of the cell, knows he hasn't a clue what it means.

Tim imagines Vera laughing at his little revelation.

—But she wouldn't.

That was the problem with Vera. She was far too sincere.

She worked at life as though it were a craft, something to be mastered.

—Exhausting.

Tim had found Vera exhausting. He couldn't keep up. He can see her now, leaping up in the middle of the night, racing to Mischa before he even heard him cry; can see her hands always there, catching their baby before he fell, even when Tim was looking after him.

—She never let us work it out.

Tim hates her for that.

He stands. Kicks the bucket across the cell. Paces. The heat is unbearable. He wonders why the hell he's thinking of Vera so much. He's succeeded really well in not thinking much about her for years. The hair on his body prickles. He scratches, thinks of small mites breeding. Scratches again. Scratches until his nails dig in and scrape away skin.

He tells himself to stop, or he'll never stop. Concentrates on breathing. Hell, he remembers, is just a state of mind. He stops pacing. Looks at the four dead bamboo walls of his cell.

'This hell is real.'

Tim hurls his plate of food across the room.

Captain Rhyder is in his study.

He holds a photo in his hands. Feels his thumbs big on the slight slip of snapshot paper that holds the image of his grandson.

It was his wife who thought to ask Bob about the boy. How long they could wait until they told him. How long it would be until Tim's story hit the news.

Twenty-four hours, that's what Bob had said. He

thought he could buy them twenty-four hours. Said the eyes of the world were busy with Kosovo and the surviving African hostages. He said they were sending someone, said they should know more by then, agreed there was no point in upsetting the boy needlessly. What he meant was that in twenty-four hours they should know whether Tim was still alive.

The Captain runs his thumb across the photo. Imagines the face he cannot see. Feels the loss of too many hugs. Until suddenly it occurs to him that for all he knows he could be holding a photo of the dog. His wife put the photos there. In different shaped frames. Told him what they were. Perhaps she lied. She could have. He'd never know.

It's three-thirty in the afternoon. The Captain pours himself a drink.

Mischa finds spiders in the back garden.

He's worried they'll bite his little brother, Sweany.

'Don't let him play there,' he snaps at Vera.

'It's alright, honey. They're not poisonous.'

'I don't care!'

Mischa picks up Sweany and carries him to the back porch.

Vera watches the awkward, responsible tenderness of her eldest boy towards his little brother. A good man is what she sees, and a troubled boy.

Mischa feels her head towards them, thinks she'll take Sweany. She doesn't. She leaves him to Mischa, sits on the back step, rolls herself a cigarette and looks up at the sky.

'Red at night, shepherd's delight,' she says.

Mischa looks up too.

'Is it just the spiders?' she asks.

Mischa shrugs.

Vera's careful not to speak again too quickly, lets the noise of Tild playing in the front yard settle around them.

'Fear's a funny thing. Sometimes he gets so close I can feel him standing behind me. Just over my right shoulder. He wears a hat and grey plaid suit.'

Mischa looks at his Mum. He can tell by her face she's serious. They both crack up.

'Doesn't hurt to pay him a bit of respect,' she says still laughing.

Sweany screams, ignored, he's trapped his foot between step and verandah.

The day is endless.

Minutes implode with the weight of an hour and an hour becomes an eternity. Tim lies on his side, trying to drift through the hours without thought.

His thoughts frighten him. They don't fit how he sees himself. He tries to block them out with mantra. Any mantra.

The food he threw across the room begins to ferment in the heat. The sweet smell wraps itself around him. His stomach growls. He feels the weight of his body, heavy against the floor. He is filled with hate. Could kill. Imagines snapping the Boy's neck. He knows what it would feel like. He used to hunt rabbits.

—To fall from grace.

Now Tim understands what those words mean. His beliefs seem like stars, so far above him he can no longer touch them. He thinks of Mischa and tears run down his face.

He rolls onto his back. Daylight is withdrawing from

the cell. A dog barks. He allows his eyes to close. Men pass, talking softly. Tim plots, like a star map the sounds and voices he hears, even after he has fallen asleep.

Tim wakes with a start to a silent world. The cell is black-dark. The oil lamp in the corridor has died. Tim can smell how the flame has burnt the wick, when there was no more oil to draw up through its core. He sits, draws his knees to his chest. It's cold.

He wraps his blanket round him like a shawl. The blanket is damp, has the slight smell of mould about it. Moisture beads on the unsealed pores of the bamboo walls. Bacteria is growing in the droplets of moisture. Tim feels unclean. He tells himself it's just monsoon madness.

—The pressure.

—The build-up.

—The weight of water in the air.

He is talking in his head. Talking to himself. His shoulders and neck ache. His spine aches, the damp is in his bones.

—People get sick in monsoon.

—Really sick.

—They get hot. Sweat.

—Bugs breed.

—Then it gets cold.

To Tim the quiet seems unnatural.

—Maybe they've gone.

—Left me.

He searches the night with his ears. Nothing. No voices. No footsteps. No dogs barking. He feels the now familiar grip of panic tighten across his chest. Breathes down the impulse to bash on the walls. Scream. Wake someone up. Anything just to know they're there. That someone's there.

Reason tells him his fear is irrational. Reason is all he has. He listens hard.

—Nothing.

And then he hears it. A pulse. A familiar rhythm.

'Frogs. Great. Just me and the frogs.'

Suddenly bitten, Tim slaps the side of his face.

'And the mosquitoes.'

—Malaria.

'I'm going to die of malaria.'

Tim can see it. Days will pass. He'll be delirious. Fever-ridden. Desperate for water. No-one will come. Because they are dead, or gone, but he'll never know because he can't get out. Only the frogs that come with their little suckered feet, to peer in at him through the bamboo bars, will know. And they won't tell him. They'll just turn around free to go when they're ready.

Suddenly an overwhelming hatred of frogs comes upon Tim. He tries to laugh it off. Stands. His knees crack loud against the silence. But it isn't funny.

—If a tree falls in a forest and no-one hears it, has it made a sound?

The old remembered question comes to mind.

—And if I scream and no-one hears?

Tim doesn't know the answer. Ghosts pass through him. A choir of unheard screams. Fear sends currents down his spine, makes his skin crawl. He sees himself telling his father he's sick of his war stories.

'You're always going on about your mates and the war. On and on about your fucking mates.'

His father punched him then. Knocked him out. That

was seven years ago, and other than hello, they haven't had a conversation since. It had been the last straw. A slap at fifteen had been one thing. But a punch at thirty-four had been something completely different. That was the day Tim lost the last vestige of respect for his father.

Tim looks around the cell, empty, except for him.

Wonders if he'd have seen the punch coming if he hadn't looked away. No. He couldn't have imagined this hell before. Couldn't have read the real meaning behind his father's stories about his mates.

Tim rests his head against the damp grain of the bamboo wall. Wishes his father had just said what he meant. He looks out at the night through bamboo bars. Freedom is only a few feet away. He thinks of Mischa. Hopes he's OK. Hopes no-one's told him. Doesn't want him to worry. The muscles knot in Tim's stomach.

—Of course they'll fucking tell him.

Vera tells him everything.

The walls of the cell begin to close in. He's not good at saying what he means, even to himself. He wants to hit someone. As a child emotion gave him asthma.

'Gotta make a plan. Gotta think clearly.'

He begins to pace. He's only fifty-nine miles from the border.

—Not even that if I go as the crow flies.

—Across the mountains.

He can see it in his mind. Maybe it's only twenty miles. He's just got to get out.

—The river!

The idea comes with a rush.

—I can get away at the river.

He remembers the river is wide. That white light reflects

off the water. He can dive down deep. Get away from the bullets. He can feel the possibility. He'll find a reed, breathe through it. Tim slows his mind down. There are things to consider.

First there is a knock.

'John! It's Ben. Come on mate, unlock the door. Let me in.'

The Captain has no idea how long he's been in his office. The first half bottle didn't even touch the sides. He stands. Holds himself steady with the tips of his fingers. He remembers his wife bringing food. He told her to fuck off, he wasn't hungry. That had been a long time ago.

'John!'

'Yeah, yeah, yeah!'

Ben never had been patient.

The Captain knows it's only a straight six paces from the edge of the desk to the door but tonight it seems a long way. He lets go of the desk and steps out into the room. Into the space between objects. Actually he makes it across the room rather well, considering. Only a few feet off. He unlocks the door and heads back towards his chair before he falls over.

The Captain hears the click of the light switch. He hates it when he forgets to turn on the lights. For sighted people it's such a pathetic image. Even if you're reading, they don't know. He smells coffee.

'Not like you Ben.'

'It's not for me. I'm having a scotch.'

'No you're not. The scotch died hours ago.'

The Captain laughs. Ben puts the coffee into his hand. He sways.

'Maybe you better sit down first.'

The Captain sits. Ben wraps both his mate's hands around the coffee mug.

The Captain listens. Follows Ben's movements while he pours himself a drink. Sits. Then there is silence, marked only by sipping, and the hum of traffic.

'Joan told you then?'

It's the Captain who breaks the silence.

'Yeah.'

'Here's to 'em eh? Cheers!'

The Captain raises his mug, tipping it sharply. Warm liquid spills down his hand, leaks between his fingers.

'Cheers,' says Ben.

They meet mug to glass. The Captain's face puckers as he takes a swig of his coffee.

'So bloody sweet!'

'She's worried about you.'

'Touché.'

The Captain turns the mug in his palm. Feels the grain of the china in the unglazed base.

'Want something in it?' asks Ben.

'Is the Pope a Catholic?'

Ben gets a bottle from the sideboard.

'How much have ya had?'

'Don't know. Can't see remember. How many empties are there?'

'Too many.'

The Captain laughs. Ben spikes his coffee and pours himself another drink.

'You try and tell 'em the war's not over,' he says.

The chair squeaks as he sits.

'They don't listen,' says the Captain. 'It's all peace, love and fucking mung beans. But nothing's changed.'

'They're bastards John. We know, we fought 'em.'

The Captain swallows. Tears he's never cried threaten. His head swims. He's drunk too much. He wishes he knew what his son looked like. As a baby Tim had curly hair. The Captain remembers that. And that his mother adored him.

'It'd be really cruel,' he says, in a voice tired with restraint. 'If she lost him and was left with me.'

Ben knows the truth of it. His wife left in '64. Said he was different. But Joan stuck it out. Never said a word. Ben takes a sip of brandy, stares into the bottom of the glass.

'Better you than no-one John.'

The Captain smiles.

'That's the problem, isn't it.'

When the Boy comes, just on dawn, Tim is ready.

The Boy takes in the food sprayed across the cell.

Tim smiles. Sits the sack on his head like a hat and picks up the bucket.

The Boy points his gun at Tim's chest, suspicious.

Tim pulls the sack down, covers his face. His father'd like the Boy.

—'Never underestimate the enemy.'

His father's words.

From the doorway of the cell Tim counts his steps. Sixteen down the corridor to the outer door. About seven metres. Pacing his cell he's worked out, if his steps are small, he takes two to the metre. The Boy guides him through the doorway, his gun at Tim's back. Then left along a path that veers right into the jungle. It is one thousand and fourteen steps to the river.

—About a quarter of a mile.

Tim smiles to himself, feet to metres, metres to miles, kilometres only when that's how far he's told something is. And then he still converts in his head back to miles. The mark of a confused generation one foot in both camps.

A quarter of a mile means a couple of minutes. Tim hopes that's right. That he has a couple of minutes after he makes a break before anyone can reach them. Standing on the edge of the river, his feet sinking into the mud, his heart beating uncomfortably fast, Tim doesn't think a couple of minutes sounds like very long.

The Boy pushes Tim to kneel. He doesn't. He squats. Pulls the sack from his head. He'll make his break when the Boy's distracted. The first light of morning dances bright on the water. The shallow water. The white he remembered was the reflection of light off shale. Shale blanketing the bed of the river, not a foot down.

Tim begins to laugh. He can see himself standing in the middle of the cell, eyes bright, breathing fast with the thought of escape. Who was he kidding? If he'd tried to breathe through a reed he'd probably choke on a slug. He's seen too many James Bond films.

And now he's crying. Laughing and crying.

—Like a crazy man.

The whole thing is crazy; the day; the mist rushing to meet the sun too fast; his hands in chains; the dirt under his nails; the Boy with a gun, aimed at him. And he can't stop laughing.

The Boy orders him to stop.

He lifts his hands, a gesture of compliance. Tries to explain. Share the joke. Words come out, pitched high. Squeezed thin by laughter.

'I thought the river was deeper.'

He steps forward without thinking.

The Boy shoots.

Tim's not laughing now.

Someone calls to the Boy from across the river. The Boy answers. Tim stares at the ground where the bullet hit. There'd have been no head start.

—'Never underestimate the enemy.'

Tim looks at the Boy.

The Boy's eyes don't talk. Tim can't read him. He focuses on a scar high on the Boy's left cheek, near his eye. Remembers the Boy has another scar, across the back of his right hand. It's puckered, twisted like rope. Tim has a scar, on his knee. He fell off his bike once.

Back in the cell, Tim pulls the sack from his head and turns to the Boy.

'Why?' he asks, 'Just tell me why.'

The Boy closes the door without a word. Bolts it.

Tim imagines the pleasure of that small cruelty. He's closed doors on people; mostly women. The sound of the Boy's footsteps receding underline the insult. Tim turns from the locked door as though there were somewhere to go. There isn't.

His lips curl in a silent snarl. His breath drags with it the almost inaudible moan of an animal. He kicks the wall. Already the heat is building. He kicks the wall again. Runs his fingers through his hair, pushes it back off his face.

There's fresh food in a bowl by the sleeping mat, and yesterday's mess has been roughly cleaned away. Tim stares at the water marks, imagines the woman kneeling on the floor of his cell. It's been days since anyone spoke to him.

—Lonely.

The feeling wraps itself around him. The day has only just begun.

Tim tries to ignore the tension in his belly. Squats. Picks up the bowl. Like a monk, he'll eat half now, half later. Each mouthful, rolled neat between his fingers. Offered for the benefit of all beings.

He chews slowly, thirty times, tries to be in the moment. Tells himself it's good to eat slowly.

—Chew your food.

The moment distorts, loops Tim back in time.

—Vera doesn't chew her food properly.

—Drinks orange juice when she eats.

—Lets Mischa do the same.

Frustration knots his stomach.

—It's bad for the digestion. Why can't she see that?

He's still hooked in there. But she's with someone else now.

—Living a different life.

And so's his son.

Tim suddenly feels a sense of distance. His heart pounds hard against feeling like a metronome. The irony is cruel, the passing of time is measured in heartbeats. Each one taking him further away from then; when they shared a life together. He's never thought about it before; what it meant to separate.

—And now it's too late.

He and Vera don't even recognise each other any more.

—Every cell in their body is different.

Tim thinks of his mother and father. Their wedding photos. And then of his mother's face the day his father shot the dog. The horror in her eyes. She hadn't married that man. She married someone kinder.

Tim can still see his father holding the dog's head down with his foot. His pistol to its skull.

'A blind man shooting a blind dog.'

Tim summarises the event in seven words. It's his body that remembers he wished someone would shoot his father.

Tim puts the bowl of rice down. He doesn't want to know that about himself. Doesn't want to remember that. He wishes this all would stop, so he could just stop thinking. The real hell is in his mind. He's got to fill in the time. Do some practice. Three sessions.

—Let it all go.

—Turn the other cheek.

—It'll be alright.

Tim feels the two beliefs fit together within him, like the two halves of a ring. He hears the Dharma with Christian ears.

He wonders suddenly what that means. When he sits in a gompa surrounded by Tibetans for a teaching, are they even hearing the same thing?

—Which parts of a teaching do Tibetans cling to?

—Do they take as fact things I hear as parable?

Tim wonders how converts from other religions hear the word of God. Surely not the same way his father does. His father is a Christian. Wears a cross around his neck. Tim's never seen him pray.

At four in the morning the Captain wakes on the couch. He doesn't remember how he got there. He's thirsty and hot; burning hot. He staggers to the kitchen, drinks from the tap, splashes water on his face. But it's not enough. His body's on fire, his shoulders and arms are burning, his chest and the back of his neck. He is unnaturally hot. If it were day he would burst into flames, self-immolate. The heat in his body drives him to water and the shower, where he crouches and tries not to think of hell. He isn't a religious man. He doesn't believe in God.

— No. Only hell.

The voice of truth. He knows the smell of flesh burning. The Captain rocks a little. Tells himself he's still drunk, that there are reasons hard liquor's called fire water, that it'll be alright in the morning. But in the last hours of night before day, time curves back upon itself and under the running water of the A.V. Jennings shower, the Captain is beset by ghosts and demons. He wins no battles, makes no sense of anything. He simply gets through the night.

Incarceration makes Tim think.

It's terrifying. He can't seem to agree with himself about anything. He tries to keep himself busy.

He makes four marks, with his thumbnail, on the bamboo wall near his sleeping mat.

—Four nights.

He thinks that's how long he's been missing.

Tim goes over the few facts he knows about his own abduction. Constructs for himself a visual overview, a kind of map. Somewhere, fifty-nine miles south-west from where he is now, is the place where all this started. Tim reverses the image in his mind. Fifty-nine miles north-east from that point, puts him in Burma. At best, the border was only thirty miles from where he was taken. And they walked for a day before the truck. Tim wonders what happened to the river. If he's right they have to have crossed the Salween.

—When?

—Before I was conscious.

He wonders how they did that. Did they drug him? Is that why he felt so bad when he woke? Why his head is leaking thoughts and images? Perhaps they went another way. Not north-east at all. But Tim can't see it. He is lost in the simplified geometric image that is to him a map. A red circle; the point of his departure. A long, thin, black diagonal line; the journey. Cut, by a short diagonal, a quadrant; here.

—Abstraction.

The word is more a realisation than a thought. It's born from a feeling in his belly. Tim actually sees a door in his mind open and abstract image after abstract image pour out. All the paintings he has seen and stored in a forgotten room of his consciousness, due to lack of understanding, are suddenly accessible. He understands the language. He can draw now. He can feel it. If they'd give him pen, paper.

—Or charcoal.

—I could make charcoal.

Tim looks at the bamboo walls. He could draw on them. Cover them. He could work. Not waste the time.

—That would change things.

Tim has to smile. He's had twenty years to work and now when he can't, he finds the inspiration. He wonders how many images the human mind can store.

By mid afternoon the cell is a sweat box, alive with madness. The air is charged with the building pressure of the coming monsoon. Only once does Tim hear voices. He calls out. No-one replies. Twice he hears dogs barking. By mid afternoon Tim prays for the sound of rain. Between the heat and the strands of himself he thinks he will go insane.

He keeps imagining breaking the Boy's neck. They are alone by the river; they are alone in the cell; they are alone. The knowledge of what it would feel like is in his hands. Tim is horrified until he becomes numb.

After that he simply understands the rage of psychopaths. They're bored. They bore themselves. There are only so many bodies one can dissect before it loses meaning. Like everything else, cruelty becomes mundane. Tim breathes out three short sharp breaths. He scares himself.

—Not a good man.

He's not a good man! The voices in his head start.

—The Dalai Lama's a good man.

Tim met him once.

—Kind. Really kind.

—To that old Tibetan woman.

—To me.

Memory pauses. Tim has a clear image of the Dalai Lama's eyes.

'Compassionate.'

—Even to me.

Tim is seeing he and the old woman standing side by side to meet the Dalai Lama. Her face is twisted, scared. She is one of the Dalai Lama's people. His responsibility. Her problems are real. She is a refugee.

—And still he made time for me.

Tim feels honoured. She must have been scared. He understands that now.

'I am scared,' he whispers.

Curling on the sleeping mat, Tim tries to disappear. Let the nothing take him. Swallow his soul. He doesn't care.

Night brings with it drunken voices. Not many, only two or three. Voices that explode in the quiet with sentiment.

—Like overfed frogs.

Tim feels the threat, that they might come to him, want to play.

They don't. The night ends with slurred voices raised in a song that peters into silence. Tim is left with the tension of an unrealised threat in his belly. Carries it with him into an awkward sleep.

The phone rings.

The Captain's wife beats him to it.

'Hello!'

It's five-thirty in the afternoon. There has been no news all day. The Captain drowns in silence while his wife listens.

'So there's no news,' she says.

Her tone is curt. The Captain exhales, at least he knows.

'But about Tim there's no news?'

His wife's run out of patience. He knows she's cut Bob off.

'You better talk to my husband,' she says.

She doesn't care about the delicate politics of the region. Doesn't want to hear excuses. Just wants news of Tim. She hands the Captain the phone.

Men don't understand. The small injustices are hard enough to swallow. It's been nearly a year since Joan saw Mischa. The Captain doesn't like going to Melbourne. Too many memories. It's where he was sent home, to repatriate. Joan breathes down her anger.

No, she doesn't want to hear excuses. She'll go and find Tim herself if necessary. She thought about it all through the night, while the Captain fought his battles under the shower. She thinks it was cruel to leave him, but she'd had enough. She needed a plan. Something real to fall back on.

Joan knows she's not a worldly woman but she isn't stupid either. She doesn't trust the system to save her son. The Captain hangs up.

'Tim's been taken by Burmese Communists.'

He almost laughs.

'Some group I've never heard of.'

'Why?'

The Captain shrugs.

'But why Tim?'

Something in the Captain snaps.

'He's white!'

The Captain doesn't hear his wife begin to cry because there is no sound. And he can't see the tears run down her cheeks. He simply falls into the hole of her silence, accused.

The Captain knows she will leave him when all this is over.

He breaks the silence. Spits out the information that Tim's abduction will be on the news tonight.

'We've got to ring Vera!'

The Captain hears Joan's panic, each word is clipped. He didn't mean to do that to her.

'Mischa musn't find out from the news. Not from the television!'

'No. Of course not.'

The Captain can't make the call.

'You better phone,' he says.

Vera's hands shake as she hangs up the phone. She feels quite sick. Her stomach rises up to swallow her heart. Outside it is sunny. The street and the yard are framed in the doorway. Mischa is happy today.

Angry, Vera slams the front door. Shuts out the street. The simple life she has just begun to trust. Fuck Tim. She'd like to rip out his heart. She doesn't want this for Mischa.

'Oh.' A small sound escapes her.

She doesn't want this for Tim either.

Her lungs hurt. She's holding her breath. She makes herself breathe. She can't think about Tim now, she's got to think about Mischa.

Giggles come from the lounge room. Mischa and Tild and Sweany watching *Rug Rats*. Adults don't giggle, thinks Vera. They laugh, it's different. Tears well in her eyes. She's got to tell him.

She needs a cup of tea and a joint. Wishes Joe was home. She's got to think this out. Doesn't want to make it worse than it is. To get to the kitchen she has to walk through the lounge room.

'The hallway's a stupid place to have a phone.'

Vera wipes her tears away with the back of her hand.

More giggles.

She isn't going to tell Mischa tonight, that much she knows. She's going to put bubbles in the bath, make them body paint with soap and they are going to have a good night.

All night Tim's mind is filled with Mischa. Images slowly unravel into dream. It is late spring. They are on the veranda. Tim looks out at the lawn. Mischa is beside him eating dinner. The grass is high. Tim wonders when it grew so much. They'll have to get someone in to mow it. Mischa looks up at him.

'Why me here?' he asks.

Tim isn't prepared for the question. Doesn't have an answer. He falls through the pool of his son's eyes into another life.

Mischa is eight. The country is at war. It is another time. Another place. Somehow Tim knows it's France. That he is in the Resistance. That everyone's been taken. He is Mischa's father. All Mischa has. And he is angry. Angry that they could do this. He cannot tolerate the injustice. He skirts a path through the rubble of a bombed city back to Mischa. Back to the others. The worse the war becomes, the harder they will fight.

They are in the country before Tim realises Mischa is not with them. No-one else seems to notice. They are on a mission. Tim is worried. Wishes he knew where Mischa was. But it's too far to go back. It'd take too long. He can't slow the others down. He says nothing. Tells himself that Mischa will be alright, and in his mind places Mischa in the kitchen of friends. People are dying. They have a war to fight.

But when they arrive it is already too late. The camp is deserted. Everyone gone. Desperate Tim and his comrades search the empty sheds. There are friends among the prisoners. If possible they will have left some word, some clue, as to where they have been taken.

Tim drags the old barn door open and freezes. Stares in horror at the hundreds of jumpers nailed to the wall. Skins of victims. Each jumper marks a life. A man's. A woman's. A child's. Tim thinks he will be sick. And then he sees it. Mischa's jumper. The one his mother knitted for him before she died. And Tim knows he did this to his son. He left him unprotected. Tim screams. But there is no sound. The scream is trapped in him.

When he wakes there is a hurricane of feeling in his chest. He doesn't remember his dream. Only knows that anger is caged in him, and he is caged in this cell. He kicks the wall.

'Fucking bastards! Gooks!'

He kicks again, nearly breaks his toe.

'Jesus!'

Tim rubs his foot. Gooks, is his father's word. He doesn't think like that. He remembers Lenny. A friend he made one Christmas when his family went camping up north. He really liked Lenny. Lenny was Aboriginal. Taught him stuff. That was a good summer. He's not like his father.

When the Boy comes, Tim's smile is genuine.

At the river he takes his time. Talks to the Boy. Holds up chalk stones. Tells the Boy he could draw with them. That he's an artist and that's what he does, draw.

The Boy says nothing.

'I have a son,' says Tim, 'Bit younger than you.'

He wants the Boy to know this. Wonders if he understands. The Boy makes Tim drop the stones and finish washing.

They walk back to the cell in silence.

—So begins another day.

As the cell door closes, Tim's new-found equanimity shatters. He throws himself against the door.

'Talk to me!'

There's no answer. But there's no sound of footsteps either. The Boy is standing on the other side. Held to the spot. Tim can feel him standing there.

'Come on,' he says. 'Say something! Anything. Doesn't matter if I don't understand.'

Silence.

Tim tries humour.

'You could always tell me where I am!'

The Boy shifts his weight.

'It was a joke! Sorry. Just a joke.'

Tim thinks he's lost him. Thinks the Boy understands. Is just pretending.

'Jesus Christ say something. Please.'

The Boy turns and walks away.

'Yeah, well fuck you too!'

Tim turns, walks through himself as he takes two paces to cross the cell.

—Really clever Tim.

—Blew that one.

He didn't mean to snap. Meant to reel the boy in. Win him over.

—Really fucking clever.

He stops, nose against the wall. Always there are voices in his head, bickering.

—Yeah, but the voices are you dickhead.

Dickhead, mate, arsehole. He's so Australian. Not how he talks, how he thinks. She'll be right is in the grain of him.

His stomach growls. His body's picked up the scent of food.

'An egg!'

It looks so perfect. He'll save it till last.

—Why not eat it first?

—No-one eats the best thing first.

—Some people'd eat it first.

—Who?

'Jesus!'

Tim holds his head. He can't even agree with himself about when to eat a lousy egg. He'd like to smash that bloody door down. His body's instinct is to throw something.

—Not the food!

He laughs.

Tim likes that part of himself, the pragmatist. It's the other voices he's not so sure about. He wonders suddenly if he'll die soon.

—Soon is a relative concept.

Like that voice.

—Pompous ass.

The strands of his personality have begun to separate in the heat. He begins to rock.

—That's right do it properly.

—Mad people always rock.

What is it his mother says?

'If you can't do something properly, don't do it at all.'

He smiles. Talking's better. At least it's a real voice.

Tim wonders how many voices there are in his head. How many people he carries around. No wonder he can't make up his mind about anything.

—No, that's not true!

—Sometimes I know things.

—The occasional voice of God.

He laughs. Then feels his heart palpitate. Why did he say that? He doesn't believe in God. Doesn't want to find God now in a moment of crisis. Be too pathetic. He stops rocking. Imagines the walls of the cell graffitied with the symbol of anarchy.

—A rebel in your own mind.

Suddenly his father's voice is in his head.

Tim doesn't want to think about him, it's easier to think about God. He looked the word up once.

—A superhuman person.

The definition struck him as somehow odd, it allowed possibility, unlike the church. Tim bites at the dry skin of his lip. Ruminates over the idea that belief in God stems from an encounter with aliens. Images of Charlton Heston in a toga pass through his mind. He really is going mad. He rolls his head to loosen tension.

—There could be something to it.

He scratches at his beard.

Sitting in a cell Tim finds it easy to imagine that all the killing in the name of God, all the religious wars, have actually been fought for the greater glory of one, green, multi-digited being, over another. That the universal function humans perform is of keeping peace in the rest of the universe, while annihilating themselves.

—Each side chooses a team to fight for its interests.

—Fuels them with doctrine.

—And then sits back and watches them go for it.

—Battle it out.

No matter who wins, humans lose.

Tim is straddling a line of irreverence and sincerity. He glimpses the superstitious nature of humans as a species. Hears his father quote Sun Tzu.

> —'Supreme excellence consists in breaking the enemy's resistance without fighting.'

Humans are easy to break. Suspicious, frightened of difference. Even as a child Tim knew not to bring Lenny home. The sins of the father. There is a line, even now, he can't cross. He doesn't have the right to say, 'Please teach me about my land.'

Tim picks up his bowl and begins to eat, takes a bite of the egg. A thought crosses his mind.

—Could you be a Tibetan Buddhist if you were Chinese? Dry, the yolk sticks to the roof of his mouth. He washes it down with warm mint tea, a strange taste sensation for him. What he'd really like is a beer. Taking a ball of glutenous rice between his rough man's fingers Tim understands why people believe in God. It makes things so much simpler. Belief doesn't require proof.

Tim thinks of Vera. After all these years he can still picture Vera's face without even trying. He runs his fingers through his hair, massages his scalp. His brain strains to grind over the coarse particles of his own feelings.

Sweet mango lassi, and Vera laughing, meringue on her nose.

—So pretty that day.

—Didn't tell her though.

—Didn't want things to get serious.

—They just did.

Tim leans back against the wall.

—It's true.

—Fool youth.

That's what Rimpoche's father always calls him. Now he understands why. Can pin-point the moment when he was supposed to grow up.

He and Vera were in India. They hadn't slept for twenty-four hours. Their train had been lost somewhere. Tim refused to leave the station in case it came and they missed it. They were already a day late. And he didn't want to miss the Kalachakra initiations.

He remembers handing Vera a cup of chai, noticing the tears running down her face and wondering if he could get away with not noticing. But she'd been too quick, she'd started speaking. And so he'd sat down beside her, the bubbles of her words bursting about him unconnected.

He caught, 'I love you.'

Returned the ball, 'I love you too.'

He was trying. Fielding close in, silly mid-on. But she hit the next for six.

'What are we going to do?'

And a hole opened up in the ground between them.

'Wait for the train,' he said.

Hoping the hole would close.

'That's not what I mean.'

Vera's words had an edge. He remembers her eyes. They could swallow a man's soul. Fear, that's why he'd snapped.

'How the fuck do I know? Jesus, Vera!'

Fear was what blew apart his lips, let his breath puncture the air with those words. She reached out again.

'I believe in you Tim.'

'Well don't!'

Her tears ran then. Time froze. There was an instant, before she turned away and started to collect her things, when he could have said something. But he didn't. He let her go. Even though she was pregnant.

'Your Dad's got himself into a bit of trouble.'

Vera looks at Mischa over the top of the Rice Bubbles packet. It's raining outside.

'Is he OK?'

Vera moves the Rice Bubbles, clears the table between them.

'I think so,' she says.

Mischa's not hungry any more.

'He was on his way home,' she says.

She wants Mischa to know this. To understand his father loves him.

'On time for once.' She makes a little joke.

Mischa smiles.

Vera's thought about it all night. The best way to tell him. To weave a truthful hope. Mischa listens. Understands everything she says. Understands the words. Hostage is a big word. They say it on the news and in films about other people's lives. He listens until the sound of the rain on the roof becomes so loud he can't hear her any more.

Vera squeezes Mischa's hand. He's disappeared somewhere inside and she wants him back. He knows he's supposed to do something. Cry, hug her, something. But his heart and his head and his gut seem to have gone in different directions and his ears are filled with the sound of rain.

'Mish, it'll be OK.'

Vera is kneeling. Looking up at him. He nods. A thousand horses are galloping into his chest.

'How are we going to get him back?' he whispers, 'We haven't got any money.'

The circus comes to Tim.

He hears them outside, rehearsing. At least that's what it sounds like.

'DE/MO/CRA/ . . . DE/MO/CRA/CY.'

Over and over, until their voices come together. Cutting through the madness of the afternoon.

'De/mo/cra/cy! De/mo/cra/cy!'

And then they come. Burst into the cell.

'Dem/Ocracy! Dem/Ocracy!'

Four guards and the Boy, faces covered, brandishing guns. From the doorway, the Captain videos the whole charade.

It takes Tim a moment to realise what's happening.

—This is proof I'm alive.

He struggles to hold up one hand. Five fingers.

'Five days,' he says looking straight into the camera.

'Get me out of here!'

The Captain swings the camera down off his shoulder. His order is sharp.

'*Hey-kaung-dway, thwar-loh-ya pyi. Thwar dot!*'

The guards file out.

'Pantomime over?' asks Tim.

The look in the Captain's eye tells Tim the Captain thinks him a fool.

'*Thu-go ah-khan-htae pait lai tot.*'

He orders the Boy to bolt the door.

Tim listens to them laughing as they walk away; he is the butt of their joke. The word 'democracy' echoes in the cell. Makes Tim think.

—One life, one vote.

—Each opinion of equal worth.

He begins to pace. One, two, three, turn. He is thinking about gerrymanders.

'For democracy truth is essential.'

Turn.

'For capitalism truth is dangerous.'

Turn.

'Democracy gives capitalism its moral high ground.'

Turn.

—But we don't have real democracy. Only a semblance.

Tim stops. Face to the bamboo wall.

—So? It's better than this.

The voice is a whisper.

Tim hears a truck start up. Grind its way slowly out of the camp. The truck that brought him here is leaving.

—With a tape of me.

Tim catches his own scent. Musk meant for breeding. Remembers Rimpoche talking about the condition of being human. He is beginning to understand. Hate is beginning to leach out of him. He sits. Crosses his legs, half lotus. Daylight is fading. Another day is nearly gone.

Resting in emptiness, Tim is snagged by a feeling buried in a memory. He's fifteen. He rips the still warm skin from a rabbit. Only then does he realise what he's done and he feels slightly sick. But hearing his mates he pulls it together.

—It's hard to be a man.

He thinks of Mischa.

—Boys will be boys.

'What kind of shit is that to put on a kid?'

Tim stands. His mind races.

—Economics and politics are personal.

He can see that now. Begins to pace again. In a three-stride cell he will break the four-minute mile. It's just that he's such a small player it's taken him a long time to understand. It takes thousands like him to create the illusion of freedom.

—So others believe they have a choice.

—Will die for it.

—Lose their sight for it.

Tim's eyes are filled with tears.

—'You're a fucking idiot! No-one's free!'

Tim stops. He understands what his father had been trying to tell him.

—Cheers Dad.
A silent toast.

Feeling forms a thought. Tim thinks that a lot of the suffering in the world depends on man believing he's powerless to change things.

—But he's not.
Tim laughs. Of all the times to have had this realisation. When there's so little he can change. And then it comes to him. No-one can make him eat. If they won't tell him where he is, why they've taken him, he'll simply refuse to eat. Force their hand. Change the play.

Tim begins to dance. He dances in his cell with a flat-footed jig.

Faceless!

A faceless man. Mischa is dreaming. It's Tim, it's his Dad. But why is he faceless? He shouldn't be faceless. Mischa knows Tim's face. He does! He knows it!

Mischa wakes. His Dad, he can't remember what his Dad looks like. He sits up. The quiet rings in his ears. His room doesn't look real. Night has stripped it of colour. He's in a half world, a shadow world. He's scared and wants to run to Vera. Wants her to make everything alright. She can't any more.

Mischa lies back down, alone in the dark with his eyes open.

Shortly after dawn the Boy comes as usual.

Tim washes as usual. Everything is as usual until they get back to the cell. Tim asks the Boy to wait. Mimes for the

Boy to wait. Picks up the fresh bowl of food and hands it to him.

The Boy seems confused. Pushes Tim to take it back. Tim shakes his head.

'I want to know why. If I'm going to die, I want to know why. I won't eat until you tell me.'

The Boy shoves the bowl back at him, hard.

Tim forces his arms to hang loose in front of him. He's not going to take the bowl. He's not going to fight about it. He's just not going to take it. A look comes into the Boy's eyes. Hate.

The Boy puts the bowl of food on the floor. Leaves Tim caught in the breadth of his own stand.

'Shouldn't be too hard.'

Tim picks up the cup. Has a sip of tea. Makes another mark on the bamboo wall, six days.

Not eating is harder than Tim thought it would be. His eyes keep drifting to the bowl of food by the door. He finds himself staring at it. Fantasising about ways of taking just a little so they won't notice.

—But it's not about them.

Tim closes his eyes. Each breath fills him with the scent of food.

'Jesus Christ!'

He's going to have to breathe through his mouth. Bypass his sense of smell. He relaxes his jaw. Lets his mouth open. It helps. He concentrates on his breath. On the Samadhi of the breath. Gets stuck in the black between his shoulders. Nothing will pass through there. He can't shift the blockage. Tim doubts his meditation has ever done him, or anyone else, any good. Flashes on the fact, he's not exactly Mr Compassionate. Except when it suits him.

Tim opens his eyes, the sting of truth. Straightaway his eyes are drawn to the bowl of food. He takes a sip of tea. His stomach growls, churns upon itself like an angry child.

Mischa wishes everyone would just leave him alone. Stop saying things like, 'Your Dad's going to be alright. Don't worry,' when they don't really believe it. Mischa can see in their eyes they're lying. Not saying what they believe. All their nice words don't make him feel better. They leave him wanting to hit. To scream.

'He's not going to die! He's not!'

But he never does. The moments slip past before he recognises them. Mischa's not really there. He's lagging somewhere behind himself. And Vera seems a really long way away, when he looks at her.

The Boy comes in the middle of the afternoon, to check whether Tim's eaten. Tim smiles at him and the Boy goes away. Tim listens to him go. The Boy doesn't usually walk that fast.

—He's annoyed.

The outer door slams. In the first moments of silence comes elation.

'Yes!'

He's getting to him. He's putting a spanner in the works. Tim does a little victory lap around the cell, imagines cheers from a crowd.

'Yeahhh. Yeahhh.'

—Too hot, that's enough.

He sits. He's getting hungry, really hungry.

Revision of his multiplication tables leads him to contemplate the theory of expediential growth. He remembers the petri dish; one cell multiplies and there are two; two multiply and there are four; four multiply and there are eight; the process slow until bang! In one day the petri dish is overflowing, there's not enough room, not enough resources.

—The crucial point is half.

Tim imagines all the billions of people in the world. Sees them copulating. Feels the sweat of coupling.

—Could never make us stop.

The thought of a population explosion makes him horny. Outside gathering monsoon clouds rumble. The air is stifling, but it won't break, not yet.

—Wanky, wanky, why not.

He's nearly got through the day.

—Fight one desire with another. Create a diversion.

Tim has to admit the notion has a certain symmetry. And Hanna had such beautiful breasts they deserved to be contemplated.

Golden, firm, she was young. He'd cup them in his hands, play with the nipples with his tongue.

But he'd always wanted to push down, suck them hard.

His palms ache with imagining. He closes his eyes. Runs his hands across his chest. Now he's hard. And he's not thinking about food. He imagines pushing down on her, feeling her ribcage beneath the plump flesh of her breasts. Releasing all his strength, not holding back.

—What that would feel like.

Opening her legs and it being his right to look. No taboos. To make her cunt wet, he would play with it, open it wide and run his tongue once from the entrance of her vagina to her clitoris. She'd quiver and he'd rest his head on her thigh and watch, his breath hot, teasing her, until she begged for him.

Other images fill him, but he is seeping. He runs his thumb across the head of his penis and it is her.

He takes her from behind.

The release is good.

He drifts, vaguely wonders if he should have conserved his energy and falls into a steamed sleep.

He wakes during the night with sharp pains in his gut. Wrestling them fills in the hours.

In the morning when the Boy comes, Tim finds it difficult to stand. He's not as tough as he thought he was. He notices the Boy take in the untouched food.

Walking to the river the Boy pushes the pace from behind. They both remember. Tim smiles to himself. The Boy prods him in the back with his rifle. Tim won't be hurried. It's personal.

'He's alive!'

The light in her voice makes the Captain smile. He'd forgotten she could sound like that.

'Oh John! They've got a video. He's alive!'

She puts the receiver into his hands.

'Hello Bob?'

The Captain listens while Bob fills him in. 'They've received a video. It confirms the involvement of the Burmese Communist Minority Coalition, the BCMC. Both the

Thai police and the Burmese junta, are being very co-operative. Have passed information on to the Australians regarding their suspicions that Tim is being held in Burma. Just across the border, somewhere in Shan State.'

It's the cracks between the facts that concern the Captain. Strategy.

'What are they asking for?' he asks, cutting Bob off.

'Democracy,' says Bob.

The Captain smiles. Doesn't say anything.

'Mr Rhyder, we will get your son out.'

Bob believes what he's saying. The Captain can see his words in neon. Each letter white against the fractured black of his own blindness. Maddening, disorientating. The Captain moves his head from side to side. Tries to balance the shifting planes of light that only happen when his eyes still try and see. It had not been easy to teach himself to live in his other senses.

—Half a man.

It is taboo to say but that's how he feels, especially now.

His wife catches the thought.

'Two days without food.'

Tim marks the bamboo wall. Considers he is now beginning to lose his reason. Which under the circumstances, he considers quite reasonable. He marvels at how he's managed to make this even harder on himself. Knows there was a good reason for his stand in the beginning, the meaning, however, has become a little obscure.

Hunger, as such, is not the issue any more. He feels quite nauseous. His stomach rolls from time to time like a living thing, a serpent he calls Frank. His unfed pet. Easier to keep than a rock. When he gets home he's going to market them.

When the Boy comes to check him in the afternoon he is standing, leaning against the wall as if he hasn't a care in the world.

—Never be predictable.

Strategy he learnt from his father.

The Boy's eyes take in the untouched food. Tim swallows a smile. The Boy gone, the day is over.

—At least I've got him coming twice. That's something.

Tim runs his nails through the coarse stubble of his face. His skin is damp. Where his nails catch there is the sting of salt. He's never had a beard before.

Tim realises he's lost track of the monsoon, when it should break. He can imagine rain. The relief of it. The sound. Then bang, he's back in the fuel tank, and the sound of water is followed by the crack of the arc. He shakes his head. He's broken into a sweat. He makes himself breathe through the pounding of his heart and rationalises the experience as lack of food. Nothing more, nothing to be frightened of. However, he is filled with the lurking doubt that experience may be all there is.

After all, Coke is the real thing. His mouth waters. What he'd give for a Coke. For an instant he ponders whether Coke has replaced religion. A simpler option, myth in a can. And when you're losing faith, all you've got to do is take a drink and there it is again, the taste of a thousand advertising images and you're part of it and back on track.

'John?'

The Captain's wife takes his hand across the table. Her fingers are cold, smaller than he remembers. It's been a long time since she held his hand.

'We have to go,' she says. 'I can't just sit here and pray.'

The Captain says nothing. She pulls her hand away. Stands. Starts to prattle.

'Maybe we can do something. I don't know.'

'Like what?' the Captain snaps, 'Get in the fucking way!' He can be vicious.

His wife becomes very still, gathers herself.

'I don't know,' she says quietly. 'But I have to go.' Her jaw is set to fight.

The Captain ages as she watches him. Skin of crepe. Ashes to ashes. It frightens her. She can destroy him now. Leave him here to do nothing, and even other women won't help. There is a twisted coil that tempts her. Panic. She hasn't battled all these years for it to come to this.

'John,' she says, and her heart hurts.

She's been so cold for so long, and so right.

'I need you.'

The words are tiny on her tongue. They're true.

She leaves the room. The Captain hears her in the kitchen cracking eggs..

—On the third day he rose.

This is Tim's third day without food. When the Boy comes Tim smiles.

—Never be predictable.

Those are the words he thinks. But it wasn't that kind of smile and he knows it. The Boy takes in the untouched food. Tim slips the sack over his head. The sack is taking on the smell of him.

Outside, Tim moves off before the Boy's prod. A little joke. Focusing on his feet beneath the hem of the sack, Tim's eyes keep crossing. They are nearly at the river before he realises the Boy has let him be. Let him walk slowly. He recognises the minor victory. When he pulls the sack from his head, the morning seems exceptionally bright. He says so to the Boy.

Colour, he muses, is a wonderful thing. Perhaps he should have used more of it in his art.

—Art.

The word hangs in his mind.

—In my life.

He is thinking about Rimpoche's uncle. A political prisoner for twenty years, now always in the garden tending the flowers. And Tim understands. Wishes he'd spoken to him. But he'd been scared. Rimpoche said he was a great scholar. To Tim he'd just seemed strange.

—But there'd been torture.

Tim splashes his face with water. Sees the flat planes of light held in each drop. Realises he's going a little strange himself. Watches the water run through his fingers.

'Beautiful,' he whispers.

And a great sadness wells up inside. He would like to have given this way of seeing water to Mischa. A second cleaves in two.

Walking back hooded, the world once again reduced to a microscopic view, Tim is no longer able to distract hunger with sight. Fred, Tim's unfed pet awakens. When they get back to the cell and he smells rice, he's going to want to kill the Boy. He knows he is. The animal inside him is uncoiling. Strangling his conscience.

The sound of a truck breaks through the blanket of mist sealing the valley. Birds fly, voicing single notes of warning.

The Boy freezes. Reins Tim in to stop. Uses his T-shirt for a harness. Tim's face itches. The coarse stubble of his beard catching on the weave of the sack. Already the heat is building. Drawing sweat from Tim. Sickening. It takes all Tim's willpower not to hit out, pull free of the Boy.

—Gentle.

He tells himself. And he sends his consciousness into his ears.

The truck is coming. Grinding closer. Chewing up the silence. Somewhere to his left there is the dull thud of machete against bamboo.

A voice rings out, an order to stop. The truck keeps coming. There is a warning shot. Tim's whole body jumps. The reply is automatic gunfire.

'Jesus!'

Tim backs into the Boy. Who forces him with a grip of steel into the jungle on his right.

Branches catch and claw. Tim can't see a thing. He keeps his head down. Arms up to protect his head. The sound of gunfire punctures Tim with a syncopated rhythm. Desperate, he tries to pull the sack from his head. The Boy rides him. Gun to his back. Forces him forward. Tim slips. The Boy loses his grip.

—RUN!

Every voice in Tim's head agrees.

He rips the sack from his head. Scrambles, the earth slips away beneath him. His feet won't grip. A scream is torn from a man caught in the crossfire. Tim sweats cold. People are dying. The smell of cordite is sour on the morning air. The Boy grabs him by the hair.

In an instant the world is inverted. The Boy is on Tim's

chest. His gun digging in under Tim's jaw. Pushing his head back until his neck will break.

The Boy's eyes are shot with blood. He wants to shoot. He is shaking, sweating. Tim feels his heart move out through his bowels. Above, he hears a plane, a helicopter, something.

—Rescue!

They've come to rescue him. He knew they would. He's just got to get to them. Get away from the Boy. And then it comes. An explosion propels the Boy to hit the dirt, Tim to roll onto his stomach, shield his face.

'Jesus Christ!'

Tim's words spray out between clenched teeth. They're being bombed. It doesn't make sense.

Before the debris from the first blast has even settled there is another. Day becomes night and earth rains down from the sky. In this battering of sense Tim's eyes search out the Boy. The parameters of their war are known. This is something different. Their eyes meet. And then they hear them. Men moving through the jungle towards them. Clearing a path with random sweeps of gunfire.

The Boy is up, moving away, gun in hand before Tim realises what's happening. A voice in his head screams at him.

—This is not how you rescue someone!

—The Boy is all you've got!

And he's up following. Head down. Keeping low. Before he's had time to think about it.

'This is Radio National.'

The Captain listens to the dry voice of the newsreader. It seems to him he's been listening to that same voice his whole life.

'And now to the overseas news.'

He reaches for the packet of cigarettes he keeps in the top drawer of his desk.

'The abduction this week, of an Australian tourist in Northern Thailand by Communist-backed Burmese rebels, has sparked serious tensions in the region . . .'

—So fucking what!

'That's what they meant to do. "Feign disorder and crush the enemy."'

The Captain mutters his strategic analysis, finds his lighter.

'. . . The Thai government is threatening to expel thousands of refugees from its borders. A move supported by the Burmese military junta and heavily opposed by the UN, who have serious concerns for the welfare of the refugees. Considering Burma's human rights record . . .'

Without warning the Captain hurls the lighter across the room.

'What about the welfare of my son!'

'. . . A special envoy from Australia is currently trying to negotiate the release of the forty-one-year-old Australian . . .'

The timing of the radio announcer is so perfect the Captain almost smiles.

'. . . And now to the Middle East . . .'

The Captain turns off the radio.

'Forty-one years,' he says as though someone were listening.

Leaning back in his chair he chews the weight of decades over in his mind.

'I didn't think it had been that long,' he says.

This time to himself.

The Captain suddenly realises he still pictures himself as a young man. But he isn't. He's old, and his son isn't even young any more. He'd laugh if the truth didn't make him feel quite so ill. He reaches for the antacid in his top drawer. Grinds the cool chalky tablet between his teeth.

He can see himself, a young soldier moving forward along an unseen line, marked by latitude and longitude. A border declared in pen. The hand that held the pen could have drawn the line anywhere, and he would have moved forward. The army was all he had. He'd won a scholarship, worked hard. Was an A-grade student. This was his first time in the field. SEATO exercises. He was going to be a good soldier. The Captain remembers how the weight of his rifle reassured him. It was May 1963 and the monsoon was heavy.

In remembering, he is there again.

The word 'Quiet' is in his head. He steps forward. Half a ton of jungle litter moves forward with him. His boots are caked in mud. He stops. Leans back into the shadows of a country that is not his. Scrapes the mud from his boots with a rotting stick. Tries to quiet the racing of his heart so he can hear. Hear, before they hear him.

He wipes rain from his face with the back of his hand and suddenly he's there. The enemy.

The Captain can still feel how his breath caught. How he froze. Stared like a half-witted child, mouth open, while the rain kept falling. Maybe a minute they stood like that. Then without a sound, he was gone.

The Captain never told anyone. Didn't report sighting the enemy. Didn't want them to know he froze. A week later he lost his sight.

The Captain closes his unseeing eyes. He isn't brave.

Wanting to be wasn't enough. Losing his sight saved him from being exposed. Tears break and run down the Captain's right cheek. He wanted his son to be brave. His left tear duct aches.

—RUN!

Heads down, they run hunched. Pushing their way into the secrets of the jungle like animals. Feet slipping, faces scratched. Tim has no sense of time or distance. Only of his heart and his lungs burning to take in breath. The jungle's steep, littered. Tim's wrists are bleeding again. He holds his chains against being caught.

Sweat pours from him. The suffocating heat of the jungle is drinking from him. Two days without food and now he must run and run. The world is insubstantial. His feet slip. The jungle whips at him. The world has become the devil's playground.

The Boy disappears into a cleavage between mountains. Tim follows. Slides, uses gravity for speed. Is not careful. The floor of the gorge is damp and breeding. They scramble along its line back into the mountain.

The Boy crawls into the shadows. Starts covering himself in jungle litter. Tim falls on the Boy's legs. The Boy throws him off. Their eyes meet. The Boy has his hand on his gun.

Tim collapses against the mountain. He couldn't give a shit if the Boy shoots him. There are worse things. He closes his eyes. He would like to live through this.

In time the sound of his own blood rushing in his ears quietens and he can hear again. Hear the silence. Eerie, like a very good lie. He listens hard. Tries to remember when the gunfire stopped. Can't. He'd been running.

Sweat stings the corner of his mouth. What he'd give for a drink. A crack of thunder makes his body jump. His eyes open. Looking out, he sees clouds rolling in.

—Today?

—The monsoon's gonna break today.

This makes perfect sense to Tim.

He looks at the Boy.

His eyes on the sky. His gun is pointing at Tim.

Tim ignores the threat. Watches the clouds roll in low and thunderous. The birds and the insects. The morning has burnt all thought from him. He and the Boy sit side by side in silence.

The Boy begins to shake.

Tim looks.

The Boy raises his gun. Both hands firmly support the body of the rifle. His eyes dare Tim to make a move. Tim stares at the Boy without comprehension. He's never seen fear coiled inside another before, set to spring. He looks away.

Insects crawl across his legs. They have absorbed him and the Boy as jungle. There is lightning. In the distance there is thunder. Tim doesn't know what to do. The Boy's jaw is set against his body's shaking.

Rain brings relief. The first drops fall, heavy, almost cold. Tim lifts his face. Washes away the morning. Opens his mouth for water. Suddenly the Boy pulls at the lungi covering his face. He doesn't care any more. Fever is burning him up. He needs water. Tim realises he can feel the heat coming from the Boy.

—Do something.

Is a vague whisper in Tim's mind. His mother's voice washing through him. He doesn't know what to do. His own stomach cramps.

'Oohhoow.'

He hunches forward until the cramp passes.

—Got to eat.

He looks at the Boy.

'Go,' he says, pointing. 'We go.'

The Boy shakes his head. Almost growls. His body spasms, jerks. The Boy fights his body to keep his grip firm on his gun.

Tim can see it now, how sick the Boy is. His eyes really are shot with blood. Concern for his own health brushes the edge of Tim's mind. He's weak. Needs food. The initial relief of rain has cooled his body. Left him wet. Now he feels the chill. They've got to keep moving. He squats. The Boy raises his gun.

'Come,' says Tim.

Motioning with his head for them to go. The Boy pushes him back down to sit. Gun to his chest.

Tim feels the familiar build of anger. He looks at the Boy with such cold detachment it almost frightens him. Notices how heavy the gun sits in the Boy's hands and suddenly knows all he's got to do is wait. There'll be an opportunity. He relaxes back into the rock of the mountain.

—If the little bastard doesn't shoot me first.

Tim hears himself. Sometimes he sounds so like his father. He thinks of Mischa, always happy. Not like him.

—Doesn't live with me.

—That's the difference.

Tim feels free of responsibility. If Mischa gets screwed up it's not his fault. It's Vera's.

He looks at the Boy clutching his gun. Trying to steel himself against his body's violent shaking, and he remembers watching *Play School* once with Mischa.

—'What have we here? Three calves. Let's put them in this paddock with the cows. Mooo! Moooo! And what's this? A bull! We'd better put him in another paddock so he doesn't cause trouble.'

Tim notices the angle of the Boy's jaw cutting against the flesh and he understands what it really means. Hunger. Something physically gives in Tim's heart.

—He's only a boy and he is in a paddock with bulls.

Convulsion seizes the Boy. Throws him back against the ground, one hand still gripping his gun.

'Jesus!'

Tim tries to crawl to him. Kneels on his chains, yanks himself to the ground. Gets a face full of sodden leaf litter.

—Stupid fucking things!

He wrenches the chain free. Rolls the Boy onto his side. The rain washes the dirt on the Boy's face into his eyes. Tim's got to lift the Boy's head. Forces his hands in under him. The chains on his wrists twist. Dig into the dirt. Cut into his wrists. He drags the Boy towards him, so the Boy's head can rest on his lap. The gun comes too, dragged in the Boy's hand. Tim holds the Boy still as best he can, cradles him.

'Shhhh.'

He rocks a little and the rain keeps falling.

The Captain finds his wife in Tim's old bedroom. Senses her warm and human against the usually cool emptiness of the room.

'Yes,' she says, her voice tired, without fight.

He feels his way to the bed. That's where she is. Sits down beside her.

—Let's go.

That's what he wants to say. He feels for her hand.

—We'd better pack if we're going.

That's another way to put it.

Suddenly there is a knock at the front door. His wife swallows, she's been crying. She leaves the room before he can say anything.

Cradling the Boy, Tim loses all sense of time.

The convulsions pass. The Boy rests quieter, mumbles a little. Only when pins and needles shoot into Tim's numb leg does he think to move. He lays the Boy as gently as he can on his back. Notices the rain is easing.

—Got to get us out of here.

—Find a doctor.

Tim wonders if they're still being hunted. His curiosity is objective. Doesn't change anything. He's still got to get them out. Notices how it's easy to be brave for someone else.

He tries to pry the Boy's fingers from the gun. Delirious or not, the Boy fights him. Tim has to twist the gun from his hands. Without thinking Tim hurls it into the jungle. The Boy is burning up. Tim's focused on the Boy. Getting him to stand so he can carry him over his shoulders.

The Boy can't stand, and Tim can't get a proper grip because of the chains. He lowers the Boy back to the ground. Makes himself think. He's going to have to drag the Boy. Tim tries to get a grip under the Boy's arms. Can't. The chain isn't long enough.

—Use it.

The thought is simple. Tim lifts the Boy to sit. Catches him in a chained embrace, that hooks the Boy under the arms. Stands. Lifting the Boy, Tim feels the weakness in his back. But there's no other way. He begins to edge backwards. Drag the Boy back down the gully.

The going's slow. His feet slip in new mud. Falling backwards he pulls the Boy down on top of him. The Boy cries out. Hits out. He is fighting demons Tim can't see. Locked in Tim's arms, he is frightened. Without thinking, Tim begins to chant.

'Om mani pad me hum. Om mani pad me hum . . .'

The Boy stops fighting so hard.

Tim struggles to his feet. Drags the Boy up with him.

'Om . . . Mani pad me hum . . .'

Each syllable voices effort. The rhythm gives Tim strength. Beyond the detail of every step, of wet rotting leaves, there is something else. Tim loses himself in hope. Things can get better. Darwin was wrong. Everything is connected.

Where the gully is widest Tim begins his ascent back into the jungle. Edges backwards up the mountain. Pulls the Boy up after him.

'Om mani PAD me hum.'

The acid of his stomach is eating a hole right through him. He would give anything for food. A bowl of rice. A piece of bread. Meals he's wasted dance before his eyes. More food than the Boy has ever seen. Somehow Tim knows the balance is wrong. The world is weighted heavy on the right side.

'Om maaaani Pad me . . . Hum.'

Up is hard.

Bob tries to be gentle.

Explains something went wrong with a rescue mission.

The Captain feels his wife stop breathing.

'I'm so sorry Mrs Rhyder. Mr Rhyder.'

Bob's sincerity is unpractised.

The Captain hears his wife's lungs drag in air against her will. He puts his arm around her. She hits at him. He puts his arm around her again.

'Is there anything I can do?' asks Bob. 'Would you like me to phone your son's ex-partner? Let them know.'

The Captain feels a sinkered weight drop through his centre.

'No,' he says. 'I'll do it.'

Bob leaves, lets himself out. As the front door closes the Captain's wife begins to howl.

'Shhhh,' he says.

She hits at him, again and again. Howling she hits at him. She never says a word.

It's five years since Vera's talked to John.

At first she doesn't recognise his voice. He asks after Mischa. Tells her to give him his love. The words sound strange coming from him. She says she will. And then he tells her Tim is dead. Says he hopes they will see each other soon. Vera does not know what to say.

The Captain says he is sorry but he has to go.

'Joan needs me.'

'Of course.'

Vera is left holding the phone in her hand. Too slowly she hangs it up.

—Dead.

How's she going to tell Mischa?

'Tim is dead.'

Vera whispers the words. Tries to make herself believe them. She can't. She thought she'd know. That part of her soul would go missing if anything happened to Tim. Tears run silent. She always thought she'd know.

'He's going to be alright Mum.'

Vera jumps. Mischa hadn't meant to say anything, it just came out when he saw her crying. He is standing in the doorway. Vera's face contorts with grief.

'He is going to be alright Mum.'

Saying it has made Mischa certain.

'Oh Mischa, he's not!'

Vera's nose is running. Her eyes are running. She comes and picks him up. Wraps him around her, buries her head in the scent of him.

'Something went wrong.'

Her words drag Mischa into grief. He thinks he will drown in the warmth of her. He can't breathe. He pushes her away. Kicks to be free.

'He's not dead,' he screams. 'He's not!'

Tim can no longer feel his arms.

His shoulders have turned to jelly. He drags the Boy out of the jungle onto the tiled soil of terraced fields. Dark clouds edged in gold fill the sky. The day is dying.

—Chiaroscuro.

The word hangs in Tim's head.

He doesn't see the old man until he's standing over them. Toothless, creased, a broken red umbrella in his hand. It takes Tim a moment to place the man as help, and suddenly his body begins to shake, and hunger swells in his stomach.

—Not yet.

He's got to hold on.

'Sick. Boy sick,' he hisses. 'Very sick! You understand? Sick! BOY SICK! You help!'

The old man is suspicious.

'PLEASE!'

Tim is desperate.

The old man reaches out and touches the worn blessing cords at Tim's throat.

'Buddha?' he asks.

Tim grabs at the common ground.

'YES! Buddha!'

The old man smiles.

'Buddha!' he says again.

This time his word is a statement.

'Buddha,' whispers Tim.

He thinks he will cry.

The old man unhooks Tim's arms from the Boy. Knows to be careful. Lifts the manacles around Tim's wrists. They have cut into the flesh. Tim hadn't noticed. He sees the blood. Can't feel the cuts.

Muttering to himself the old man rips strips from his worn shirt, spits betel-juice, bandages Tim's wrists. Spits again, and begins to tell Tim what to do. To stand. To help him lift the Boy. Not like that, like this! The old man makes himself understood perfectly. He's bossy. Gnarled, and strong. He takes most of the Boy's weight.

Night takes the valleys first. They walk in a shadow world, half lit, flanked by dark. Tim loses the perception of distance. Can only take in what's in front of him. His next step.

The old man stops at the mouth of a cave. Calls out. '*Koldaw Phaylar! Koldaw Phaylar!*'

'No!' says Tim.

He thought the old man understood.

'A doctor! He needs a doctor!'

The old man ignores him. A monk has stepped from the cave.

'No! He needs a doctor!'

The monk comes towards them.

'You understand? A doctor!' says Tim. 'He's sick. Very sick!'

The monk feels the Boy's forehead, pulse. Nods as he listens to the old man.

In the dusk they stand. Four of them like ghosts gathered. Faces without detail.

In the cave, the monk lights the stub of a candle. Tim and the old man lower the Boy onto a mat. Once down Tim cannot stand. He sits, numb, and watches.

The monk is old, nearly as old as the old man. There are piles of books on the cave floor. Petchas and texts stacked on the natural shelf of one wall. The monk has been here a long time. He and the old man are friends. It's in the way the old man lights the small cooking fire, pours water from a soft drink bottle into a pot, knows where things are.

Muttering to himself the old man leaves the cave. Tim doesn't want him to go. Doesn't know why.

'He will come back.' The monk speaks in English.

Tim stares at the monk bent over the Boy, feelings stacked like panes of glass fall.

'Where am I?'

'Nainga. Burma,' says the monk.

Tim leans against the wall of the cave. Laughs. He knows where he is.

'Burma,' he says the word.

He was right. He worked it out right. He is in Burma.

The monk takes some leaves from an old tin, steeps them in the now steaming water of the pot, adds a pinch of something from a pouch he pulls from his robes. Tim watches the monk spoon the brew into the Boy's mouth. Thinks to ask what's wrong with him. Doesn't.

Little rivers of the liquid run from the corner of the Boy's mouth. The sweating and shaking are symptoms of a war he is fighting inside. Tim watches the monk tend the Boy. Sees a battle between good and evil. He has lost all sense of reality. All sense of time.

The old man returns laden.

Suddenly there is a bowl of food in Tim's hands. The old man smiles, nods. He is telling Tim to eat. He pours tea from a Chinese thermos. Tim remembers how much he likes those thermoses. The tea is sweet. He swallows. Feels that first mouthful fall into the gapping emptiness of his stomach. The monk wraps the Boy in blankets the old man has brought.

Tim feels too tired to eat until he takes the first mouthful and then he can't stop. Finished, he burps. The old man laughs. Holds up a small saw. Tim had forgotten about the chains. They have become part of him.

Tim watches. The candle splutters. The old man is good with chains, goes right through the bolt, fingers nimble. It seems to Tim to take no time.

Free, he lies on a sleeping mat the old man has brought. Wraps himself in a blanket. Closes his eyes. Simply being able to do that seems to Tim the greatest luxury.

His mind throws up pictures. He is dreaming before his body has fallen asleep. They are in a house abandoned. The old man is a pickpocket. The monk is followed by a circus. It's warm, there is a fire. The Boy is in a uniform, holding a tin soldier. Outside there is a war.

The Captain helps his wife to the shower.
His arms hurt from her punches.

'Water will help,' he says.

He'd like a shower. Like to lose himself in water. Steam fills the room, warms its ceramic cool, weights the hollow echo of his wife's sobs. Keeps them from rising. Numb, he leaves the bathroom.

Phones the doctor. Explains they've just found out their son is dead and his wife's not coping. It's what you do. The doctor will give her something to make her sleep. Take her away from the pain. The doctor says he'll be there in fifteen minutes.

The Captain hangs up the phone, goes into the bedroom to get his wife's dressing gown. Feels for it on her end of the bed. Nothing. That's where she keeps his, on his end of the bed. He thought she kept hers there too, on her end of the bed, next to his. She doesn't. For twenty years he's imagined it there.

The Captain loses the picture of their bedroom he's

constructed in his mind, and is lost. There is only black, and the threat of injury in the feather breeze that curls behind his neck. He reaches for his robe. He will take that to her. Turning away from the bed, the Captain realises he is not quite sure where the bathroom is any more. He feels his way, careful, uncertain. From nowhere comes the memory of a Christmas, a long time ago.

'Well what the fuck are you going to do? I'd already fought in a war at your age. You can't even finish a fucking course!'

'John please!'

His wife's voice.

'I don't believe in war.'

His son's long-haired words trigger a trip-wire set by the port.

'You don't believe in war. You don't believe in God. What the fuck do you believe in?'

He remembers a slightly acrid taste had replaced the once metallic zing of sixpences in his wife's Christmas pudding.

'Well?'

'I don't know.'

That's when his son told him he was going away for a while; to Asia.

'To find yourself?'

The Captain knows he spat the words.

'Something like that.'

In the silence that followed the Captain remembers feeling his son and his wife close ranks. Remembers having to steady himself because the ground seemed to pitch beneath him.

Now, fifteen years later, he names what it was he felt. Betrayed.

His son going to find himself in Asia reduced everything he'd fought for, lost his sight for, to an inconsequential twist of timing. His son was turning the very freedom he'd fought for against him.

And all his wife had said was, 'Oh John! Isn't it exciting.'

The Captain remembers leaving the room. Remembers drowning his feelings in Scotch. His anger. His jealousy. Yes, there had been jealousy. He would like to have had the privilege of throwing a pack on his back and taking off to find himself. It galled him that his own son didn't understand how easy he had it. Easy because he, the Captain, had fought to give him that right. A right he claimed with both hands as his own. Didn't even say thank you. It wasn't fair. He always thought his son would understand.

The Captain has a sense of being pulled under, into a sea he has struggled always to avoid.

—Not a good father.

Is a thought.

—Better than my father.

The Captain freezes, one hand on the bathroom door. That's how he's justified everything his whole life. Opening the bathroom door he sees himself, a weedy English boy of nine, getting off a rusty ocean liner. Walking down a gangplank, into the hot blue of a Western Australian summer unprepared. He remembers hating his father. He'd overheard a conversation. Heard something about two hundred pounds. For years he thought his father sold him. The Captain has never told his wife about his childhood. Not how it really was. His father was not a good man. The

Captain never wanted his wife to know that. Thought she might see the same tar marks on him.

In the bathroom his wife is still crying. He hangs his robe behind the door. Helps his wife from the shower. Wet, she slips from his fingers. A fish loose, back once again in the sea, while he drowns in the shallows.

How could she understand? How could Tim have understood? He never told either of them where he came from. Drowning, the Captain remembers being told, is painless once you stop fighting.

He hears her lie down on the bed. Goes and sits beside her. Waits until the doctor comes. Then he waits in the kitchen.

The young doctor does not take long. Sleep comes in a bottle, is easily administered.

'Grief,' says the doctor, 'is something else. Are you alright?'

The Captain doesn't know what to do with the question; nods.

'Well let me know how she is in the morning.'

The Captain shows the young doctor out. Turns off the lights.

Sits at the kitchen table and in the quiet dark grows gills and learns to swim under water.

There are feelings down there. Things he never knew about himself. He loved his wife. Really loved her. He was scared when he became a father. Jealous. He'd never had a mother. Was scared of his own feelings. Scared of not fitting in. The army made it easy. They gave you rules.

Lying still on the ocean floor the Captain knows he would never have made it on his own. Would never have married Joan. Would never have even met a girl like Joan in the world he came from. The army had given him a lot. At the time he just hadn't understood the price he'd have to pay. He hadn't been prepared.

Coming up for air, the Captain realises he's been sitting a long time. He's stiff, cold. Exhausted he walks to the bedroom. Lies down next to his wife. Her breathing is shallow. Quiet and broken, like a child who has been fought and made to sleep. And he remembers sitting in Tim's room, one arm through the bars of the cot, his hand resting on his son's small back.

Tim, he thinks, and there are tears.

'Not a very good father.'

He whispers the words into the down of the pillow. He'll sleep on them.

Mischa is not strong enough to swim against the tide. He is hysterical.

'I felt it! I felt it when I said it. I hadn't felt it till then. But when I said it, I felt it. He is! He is going to be alright!'

Vera tries to calm him.

'Shhhhh, shhhhh. It's alright. It is alright!'

She pushes his hair back off his face. Her hand slips across the hot rise of his cheek.

'I love you,' she whispers.

Sometimes it's too hard to swim alone. Mischa stops fighting. Sinks into the soup of breath and tears between them.

Waking to kindness,

the taste of healing herb bitter on his tongue, the weight of his head held gentle by a strong hand, the Boy is confused. He's not used to being taken care of. Tries to sit. He can't. His body is too weak. The fever has stolen his strength. He panics. Tries to fight his own weakness. Hears the words, 'It's alright. You're safe,' gentle, close.

And stops long enough to focus on the face of the man who holds him.

A holy man. A hermit. To even meet such a man is a great blessing. And here he is weak like a baby in the wise man's arms. The Boy cannot comprehend the wonder of this. The last thing he remembers is fear. The world closing in, the mud, the rain. The warm metal of his gun where his hands gripped it fast. And the face of his prisoner, clear-eyed. Waiting patient, for him to lose his battle with the black water fever that burned his eyes. Waiting for his prey to fall.

—Too tired.

Too tired to think, the Boy falls back into a dreaming sleep. Scorpions are under every rock his mother pulls. Her long fingers, callused now, brush gentle behind their striking tails. Soldiers make him put out their cigarettes with his small feet. Taunt his mother.

The Boy calls out in his sleep. The old hermit cools his brow. Chants. Draws the Boy's dreams out away from his consciousness. Blocks them, so that he can rest easy.

Each time the Boy stirs, the hermit spoons bitter herb into his mouth and replaces the poultices used to draw out fever. Until finally just before dawn the fever breaks and the Boy rests quiet.

When Tim wakes he feels shaken, fragile. As though the blood in his veins has thinned. He can hardly move his arms.

His shoulders feel as though they have been ripped from their sockets, and the cuts at his wrists swell tender and angry. He realises someone is talking; quiet words. Lifts his head to see. The monk is helping the Boy sip from a bowl.

—He's alive.

Tim hadn't actually thought the Boy would die. He'd just expected it. Wouldn't have believed he could save him. But he did. Tim sits. Pain skates across the right side of his skull into his eye. He cranes his neck to see around the monk. See the Boy. Can't. He can only see the Boy's hands, they shake when he tries to hold the bowl.

—Still might die.

Is a thought Tim doesn't want to think about.

He's got to piss. He stands. Unsteady, he walks out of the cave.

The Boy sees him leave. Is confused by what he is being told, that it was the white prisoner who saved him. Dragged him up a mountain. He remembers the push of the prisoner from behind. The difficulty he always caused in moving forward. The battle between them. The Boy doesn't understand why the prisoner would have saved him. Besides, he is white.

White people look after themselves. He's seen them in Rangoon, with their fat wallets and fancy clothes. They walked past poverty without conscience. White people think they are better than other people. Everyone knows that. Even in the army this is said. Jokes are made.

—All white people are imperialists and fascists!

This is considered a very funny joke. White people do not understand it. That is what makes it so funny. So true.

Tim pauses at the mouth of the cave. He doesn't look arrogant to the Boy any more. Only kind of big and awkward. The Boy is very touched that he saved him. And inside there is a certain shame.

The day catches Tim's breath. They are above the clouds. Here, the sky is blue. Already there is heat. And the jungle, freshly washed, is filled with sounds of life. Below, there is nothing. The world of men is buried beneath rolling fields of white. Shifting dunes that release, for an instant, secrets. Tiny rainbow stars, prisms of colour, that glint before being folded back into white. If Tim knew how, he could walk out across the clouds, lie down under a turquoise sky.

—Shangri-la.

He smiles. His lip splits. He licks it. Finds a place to piss. Safe is something he has not felt for a long time.

The low rumble of the day's building storm comes from the east. Tim feels the pressure in the air that will soon draw the clouds up out of the valley to feed the storm. He feels the pull as an etching. Paper drawing ink from metal under the pressure of the press.

—There is no Shangri-la.

Soon the mountains will be blanketed in cloud, not just the valleys.

—One world.

Mountain, valley, river, sea, everything connected.

—Jack doesn't need a beanstalk.

Tim's wrists throb with the beginning of infection.

A voice in the back of his head that has always been there, murmuring, 'it's not fair', 'what about me?', like the sound of the sea, trapped in a shell, falls quiet, and a sullen child leaves, walks out through the front of him.

Tim shakes his head. He understands freedom. It has to do with evolution. A different way of seeing things.

—'What about me?' doesn't work.

He's going to get the Boy out with him.

Tim can't help smiling. The greatest revelation of his life has occurred while he's been pissing. A whole new world order has come to him dick in hand.

'There's something in that.'

He laughs. His lip splits again.

Tim feels himself anchored to the earth. He's going to get the Boy out. He's not quite sure what that means. Where it will take them. Even if it's possible. All he knows is that he has to do this. It has to do with evolution.

The old man appears out of the mist.

'*Ha, ah-thet-shin yet shi thay da bae. Kaung-dae. Kaung-dae.*'

He is happy, happy, happy to see Tim standing, pissing.

'Buddha!' he says, and makes a fist of strength.

'Buddha,' says Tim.

The old man laughs.

He has brought food and tea. He makes Tim come, sit. The old man is not how Tim remembers him from the night before. He fusses, plays the fool. Keeps gesticulating, 'Buddha!' and enticing Tim to eat.

'Buddha,' says Tim and rolls the still warm rice between his fingers.

'Buddha!' says the old man again.

Tim nods.

—Good thing I wasn't wearing a cross.

Chanting comes from the cave. The monk is making

morning prayer. Tim looks at the bowl in his hands, dedicates his food.

'*Om ar hung.*'

—Body, speech and mind.

He always translates in his head.

The old man nods approvingly. Stops fussing, sits. The monk's prayers wash over them.

Memories from the morning before come to Tim; drops of water in his hands like crystals and then the sound of guns; the day choked with fear and bombing; the craziness in the Boy's eyes; and a line from Rimpoche's teachings, on the nature of the way things are, comes to Tim's mind.

—'When watching this world, as it seems to be,
Overwhelming despair spontaneously arises.'

Tim's eyes fill with tears.

—Men are cruel.

As a boy his father scared him. Now he scares himself.

He wonders what happened to the old woman. She was the only person who showed him any kindness. Until now he hasn't even thought about her. And for some reason this omission makes him think of Sarah, Rimpoche's wife. Her shaking hands, her tears.

—He must have known.

—Maybe she isn't like that around him.

Tim's mind pulls in strands of Vera, things he knew and didn't want to know.

—But that's me!

—Rimpoche's different.

—Is he?

Tim loses his mental footing. Slides down a mountain of shale that slices his hands, his feet.

—The curse of the teacher is the disciple.
Someone told him that once.

Behind the words and rhythm of the monk's prayers, behind the beauty of them, Tim hears the eternal signature of yearning to be a better person.

Feeling sits in his chest like a stone. Rimpoche never said he was enlightened. Only that he taught what he believed. What had been taught to him. What he tried to practise.

—It doesn't mean he gets it right.
Tim's never let himself think of Rimpoche like this before, as a man. And he remembers the rest of Rimpoche's teaching on the nature of things.

—'When watching nature as it really is,
I cannot help but feel wonder and laugh.
When the one who is laughing
And the one who feels despair both disappear.
What am I to do?'

Tim feels ill. 'What am I to do?' is the signature of a man.

Tim had wanted him to be more.

This knowledge settles with the rice in Tim's belly and the smell of the jungle. It's morning fresh already beginning to ferment in the building heat. And it's OK. Tim allows himself to go back and remember.

Ten years ago when all the sanga started whispering about Rimpoche and Sarah, Tim laughed. Told them all they were petty, didn't understand there were other kinds of love, deep and profound. Connections, not just mundane and physical.

He'd told Sarah what people were saying. What he'd said. She was grateful. Agreed with him. And they'd sat watching the sun set over the stupa, sharing a Coke. Friends. Sanga.

The next time someone mentioned something was going on between Rimpoche and Sarah, Tim got angry. He remembers his words.

> 'What's the problem? Can't Rimpoche and Sarah have a close relationship without it being sexual? Why are you all so fucking preoccupied with your genitals?'

After that most of the gossip happened out of his earshot. And for nearly ten years he floated above it. Dining with Rimpoche and Sarah. Watching videos. Going on picnics.

He reminds himself that Vera hadn't picked it either. The only difference was that Vera knew Sarah was in love with Rimpoche. When Tim tried to set her up with one of his mates, Vera said, 'Don't bother. She's in love with Rimpoche. There's no-one else for Sarah. Maybe she'll become a nun.'

And it strikes Tim that perhaps what he and Vera had in common was a profound naivety.

The thought does not take a solid form, it just sits there for a while in the sunshine, then floats away on the monk's prayers. Leaving Tim with a sense that somehow this had been the cause of so many of their problems.

He remembers the night three years ago when Sarah told him the truth. He had just arrived in the valley. Got himself a room and gone straight to the Gompa to see Rimpoche. Only to be told Rimpoche was away in Darjeeling for the next ten days. And so he went to visit Sarah. She'd been crying. He told her she should talk about it. She wouldn't. Said she couldn't. He loosened her tongue with a bottle of vodka, duty free.

He hadn't understood the push/pull Sarah described with Rimpoche. But she was very sensitive. He knew that. And he was content to listen. After everything had been said and Sarah seemed to be going round in circles, talking about this monk and that monk, and how they didn't like her, Tim suggested that what she needed was a holiday.

It really had seemed that simple to him. And he hadn't understood the look on Sarah's face, a kind of incredulous disbelief. Her child's eyes, always big, now magnified by tears.

He tried to explain. Reminded her that no Westerners stayed in the valley the way she did, all year round, year after year.

'The valley gets to you,' he said. 'A couple of weeks in Thailand with me. Things'll look completely different.'

That's when the truth came out.

'Don't you understand?' she said. 'I can't leave. I'm his wife. He's got my passport!'

Sifting feelings, Tim realises it wasn't so much the news that Rimpoche and Sarah were married that had thrown him—although their lack of trust hurt and he felt like a fool—it was that Rimpoche had Sarah's passport. Had taken her freedom. He didn't understand. Well he did. But he didn't want to. Men don't interfere with other men's business in regard to their women.

Cleaning the bowl with his fingers Tim takes the last mouthful of rice. Stares at the old man, who sits in his squat Burmese style, rocking slightly. The rhythm of a lifetime of prayer inside him. And for the first time Tim has to accept that whatever else Rimpoche is, he is Tibetan. And a man.

The Tibetans are clear about a woman's place. Tim had

somehow confused this with their regard for the mother. But Sarah was not a mother. There was no place for her at the monastery. Tim's head aches. He rubs his temples. Closing his eyes he sees barbs of wire curled across the landscape.

—Women lay them.

Not a good thought.

Tim suddenly wonders why he didn't suggest Sarah go to the embassy and get another passport. And then he wonders why she never thought of it herself. That's what he'd have done. Tim doesn't have any answers and the frustration he feels only makes him angry. What was this thing between men and women? This mess they got themselves into without even knowing, until it was too late, and they didn't have a clue how to untangle the mess, even if they wanted to.

Tim is thinking now and he realises he doesn't understand why on earth Rimpoche would have taken on the pressure of a relationship. He was a monk. He was safe. The answer stirs in Tim's groin.

—But he didn't just fuck her.

—He married her.

—It's different.

—Demands respect.

Tim doesn't know what he thinks any more.

The last time he saw Sarah she'd seemed fine. A gracious, devoted disciple, helping the monks serve Westerners tea. It comes to Tim that Sarah and Rimpoche must have been together nearly fifteen years. He can't imagine what that means. The line of forgiveness they both must walk, around each other's differences, mistakes.

—Too much shit to being human.

The battered edifice, of Tim's devotion to perfection, finally crumbles. He lets all the knowledge he's stored in his head, about the intricacies of Tibetan politics, into his heart. It does matter that Lamas fight among themselves. That linage sets itself against linage. That vows are broken. It soils the teachings.

Tim wants to be righteous. Can't bring himself to cast the first stone. The vessels that carry the teachings are flawed, human just like him.

—Coward.

The word centres itself in Tim's mind.

For the last few years he's kept promising himself he'd have it out with Rimpoche. Confront him about the situation with Sarah. He never has.

—It was never the right time.

Memory contradicts Tim's habitual position of defence.

It is late. He and Rimpoche are alone. Soft light plays across the tankas covering the walls. Rimpoche says he wonders sometimes if they chose the right child. Says he has no memory of choosing to be reborn. Outside a passer-by kicks a barking dog. It retreats in pain. Rimpoche says he gets jealous sometimes.

Tim looks out at the stupa, bathed in the light of ten thousand butter lamps. Rimpoche is asking him about the nature of his relationship with Sarah. Tim lets it slide. Mentions the full moon.

It occurs to Tim that Rimpoche is a good friend, never held his cowardice against him. From the ruins of devotion Tim feels something real begin to stir. He never really thought about what choosing to be reborn, for the benefit of others, might really mean.

—Fuck it's huge!

—If it means you have to wade through all the shit again.

—And it would.

That was part of being human. The catch. The price. Tim feels the Irish stir in him. Those genes are strong. It's the imperfection of the system that makes it so right.

If Tim uses only his head, he's not sure that it is possible to choose to be reborn.

—But if it was?

—And Rimpoche did.

He's hooked. The way only an ex-Catholic can be. And he's happy.

—There are worse things to believe in.

He can justify his faith.

—Everything is flawed.

Rice sticks to his fingers.

—Until enlightenment!

That is what he really believes.

All night Mischa dreams his Dad comes home.

He dreams it again and again. His Dad is wearing a red wool jacket and when he throws his arms around his Dad, he is pulled into the red warmth. Where the strange smell of the incense his Dad always burns still clings.

Mischa wakes pinned beneath his mother's arm.

—Not dead.

Is his first thought. And he feels the hot spring of angry tears. He pushes down into the mattress, flattens himself, slides out from under Vera's arm. The wood of the floor is cool. His feet are hot. The clock beside the bed flashes five-sixteen. Inside Mischa the horses are galloping again. He leaves the bedroom. The lounge room is better. He turns on the Nintendo. Picks up the controller. Zelda flashes onto the screen. Mischa imagines more than you see on the screen. He goes in. His thumb on the joystick takes him there.

He's up to level three. He's still a child. But soon he'll be a man. He's just got to save the Princess and find the spiritual stone of water. Then the Princess will teach him the song of time. He will sleep for seven years. And when he wakes up he will be a man. If he plays well and dies he will get another life. Mischa understands these rules. As long as he plays well.

Awake.

The Captain is slow to open his eyes. When he does he won't see anything. There will just be the same black. The same hole, which is a pit in his stomach. His wife stirs. He thinks to make her tea and toast. He gets up and goes into the kitchen. Things to do. There are always things to do.

The Captain feels awkward carrying a tray, feels unsteady. Sliding the tray onto the bedside table he knocks a glass of water onto the carpet. The powder-blue carpet his wife so wanted.

'Oh shit,' he says. 'Sorry.'

She doesn't care about the carpet any more. Says nothing.

He sits on the edge of the bed. Wonders if maybe she's still asleep. Knows she's not. He can feel the depth of her sobs telegraphed through the springs of the bed.

'I made you some tea,' he says and waits.

She doesn't answer. Doesn't sit up.

The Captain puts a hand out, feels for her. She is there. Sculpted beneath the blankets. Her back to him. He squeezes her shoulder. Leaves her to her crying.

For lunch he makes her soup. He peels an apple and cuts it into quarters. These are the things he can do. He talks with Bob at the Department of Foreign Affairs. Bob has no answers for him. No new information. Says no-one seems to know exactly what happened. Tells him two special envoys from Australia are flying into what remains of the BCMC camp later today to look for Tim's body. Says hopefully they'll know more then.

The Captain sits at the kitchen table. It is the only place he feels safe. Perched on the corner, the table leg between his legs, he knows where he is. He reminds himself that in warfare there are no constant conditions. He hears the toilet flush. It's something.

The monk introduces the old man as Tha Kin Maung. The old man slaps his thigh and grins like a fool.

'Tha Kin!' he says, and laughs. 'Tha Kin Maung!'

He puts his basket on his head, and plays a royal idiot. He's very funny.

—Silly old bugger.

The monk catches the glint of Tim's judgement.

'People are not always what they seem,' he says. 'This is an old Burmese saying.'

Tim blushes. The monk smiles. His eyes are alive with mischief. He introduces himself.

'My name is U Yewada. But you can call me Ka Daw.'

'Tim Rhyder.'

Without thinking Tim puts out his hand.

Tha Kin Maung doubles over with laughter, mimes Tim's handshaking. Tim quickly drops his hand and bows. Tha Kin Maung laughs even more.

'*Lat Oat/chi/ya/dae!*' he says, slapping his thighs.

'He is telling you we don't bow,' says U Yewada. 'We make hands like the lotus bud. Prayer hands.'

Tim holds up his hands.

'Like the lotus bud.'

They all laugh.

U Yewada's fondness for the old man floats. Tim is not sure they are all laughing at the same thing. But it doesn't matter. He sees them drawn, three axes to a wheel.

'You speak good English,' he says, not quite sure why.

U Yewada smiles.

'Thieves can steal all treasures but education.'

Tim half smiles. U Yewada's words filter through him and he notices for the first time how thin U Yewada's robes are. That his head is unshaved, and his hair tied in a tangled knot.

—A hermit. A monk in hiding?

Tim flashes on a story that has the grain of truth.

'I'm sorry,' he says. 'I didn't understand.'

'You still don't,' says U Yewada.

There is no hint of reproach.

U Yewada sits then and Tha Kin Maung serves him food. Tim watches the two old men, the delicacy of the ritual between them. Old ways. That will die with them. Sadness is textured with inevitability.

—The Boy is Burma's future.

Tim wonders what that means.

The Boy's name is Aik. Which surprises Tim. Small, brittle, not what he'd expected. Aik has malaria. U Yewada is very happy he will live.

'Last night I did not think he would,' says U Yewada.

He pauses then to eat a little.

U Yewada eats with a mindfulness that reminds Tim of

Rimpoche. Tim knows he does not usually talk while eating. He is making concession. Out of respect Tim tries to place the building rush of questions in his head to that rhythm.

'Lucky you had medicine.'

'No medicine. We do what we can. He is young, it helps. Disease is a powerful weapon.'

Tim is surprised to realise he knows what U Yewada means.

—Disease is political.

He's seen pictures of Aboriginal children with sticky eyes. Remembers the public ward at the Women's Hospital, no air conditioning, smells of blood. Memories of Mischa, newborn.

—It was far too hot.

Tim's wrists throb. They have already begun to ulcerate. The jungle will feed on him if he lets it. Tim changes gear. He can't think about those kinds of things now, he has real questions.

'Do you know who Aik is?' asks Tim. 'Why they took me?'

He hopes U Yewada knows.

'He was a soldier.'

U Yewada casts his eyes down.

'SLORC,' he says, and buries the sting of the word in his rice.

'SLORC?'

Tim doesn't understand.

'A government soldier.'

'But HE kidnapped me!'

Tim reads a certain caution in U Yewada's eyes.

'Burmese politics are complicated,' is all he says.

Tim tries to make sense of what he's being told, gather his thoughts, order his questions. Tries not to shuffle the pack.

—If he's really a soldier.

—Bad government.

—Then who bombed us?

—They had planes.

—And why me?

—Why in Thailand?

'Then who bombed us?'

Somehow Tim settles on this question.

U Yewada's smile is cold as steel.

'Only the SLORC have planes for bombing. Beautiful American planes to fight the Opium Lords. This is a fact.'

U Yewada wonders if Tim can accept what he is saying. The question is in the matt of his eyes.

After the last few weeks Tim has a sense of the nature of deceit. A black smudge in the bottom left hand corner that bleeds into lines, fine lines, almost too fine to be perceived, so that from a distance the rest of the paper still looks white. Tim will never be able to see the paper as white again. He wants to know.

'So you're saying, SLORC soldiers kidnapped me in Thailand? And then more SLORC soldiers bombed us in Burma?'

U Yewada seems to appreciate his interpretation.

'It is possible,' he says. 'Soldiers are pawns. In a game you can afford to sacrifice your pawns.'

Tim's head spins. The rains have unlocked a season's heat from the earth. The humidity is killing him, he can't think straight.

—Gotta get home!

He stamps down the rising edge of panic. His mind is doing gymnastics, trying to make sense of his abduction.

'Why would Burmese soldiers kidnap a tourist from Thailand? It doesn't make sense.'

'In Burma many things appear to make no sense.'

Tim's not really listening, he's trying to follow a thought.

'Thailand's taken in thousands of Burmese refugees hasn't it?'

He is thinking perhaps his abduction is related to this. U Yewada nods.

'But not because they wanted to. They had to. World opinion is important.'

Now Tim is really confused. He thought perhaps Burma wanted its people back. That his kidnapping was somehow related to this.

'Between Burma and Thailand the situation is very complicated. There is an old hatred,' explains U Yewada.

And then he laughs.

'One thousand years ago the Burmese Stick Army invaded Thailand. Twenty years ago when I was there, three men grabbed me and beat me with sticks. The whole time they kept saying, 'Your great, great, great, great grandfather beat my great, great, great, great grandfather to death with a stick. Now we will beat you to death with sticks.'

U Yewada rubs the crown of his skull.

'It is lucky I have a hard head.'

Tim laughs.

'But the two countries need each other. There are many . . .'

U Yewada pauses, serious now.

'. . . economic reasons. The Thai government wishes to keep good relations with Burma's military junta. But they have to be seen to be pushing Burma to be a good neighbour. A good ASEAN member.'

Tim finds it hard to understand what he is hearing.

'What does the Bo—'

Tim catches himself.

'What does Aik say?'

'That he was a soldier on a special mission. That other soldiers bombed them. That he is scared.'

'What did he say about me?'

U Yewada smiles.

'That you were a prisoner.'

Tim has to laugh.

'Not even a special prisoner?'

'In Burma, there are many special prisoners,' says U Yewada.

Tim sees in U Yewada's eyes the ghosts of a thousand men in chains, feels their breath.

'Is it really that bad?' he asks.

U Yewada nods.

'It is really that bad.'

Thunder breaks as lightning white against the sky. Makes Tim jump. Tha Kin Maung starts packing. U Yewada finishes eating. They are in rhythm with the storm that will punctuate the day. Tim is not.

'I've got to get out of here,' he says. 'Back across the border.'

His words land without grace.

U Yewada's smile is kind.

'I know,' he says.

And Tim feels the desperate edge of panic leave.

—It's going to be alright.

He hadn't actually let himself think that it wouldn't. He stored the fear. Now comes the release, the rush.

'I want to take the Boy, Aik, with me. He's too young to be a soldier.'

Tim just sort of spits the idea out. He didn't mean to put it that way.

'There are many too young to be soldiers,' U Yewada says, gathering his robes around him.

'I don't know them,' says Tim.

And he hears in his words truth. The Boy has become his rose. It's the time he's spent with him. The energy he invested in dragging him up the mountain. When Tim gets home he's going to spend more time with Mischa.

U Yewada reads Tim's face, divines the depth of him.

'In two days,' he says, 'Aik will be stronger. We can talk more.'

U Yewada stands, for now the conversation is over.

Tim can't let it rest.

'Isn't there something I can do? To help?'

U Yewada looks him in the eye.

'The boy Aik is not proud of being a soldier,' he says. 'He hates the SLORC.'

For U Yewada this explains everything. For Tim it doesn't. He is left with the familiar sense of frustration that Asia often brings him. U Yewada disappears back into the cave, the old man into the jungle. The first drops of the rain begin to fall.

Tim moves to the mouth of the cave. Inside U Yewada is with Aik. Tim squats. Looks out. Watches the rain. Watches the way water indents soil, is absorbed until it can't be absorbed any more. And then comes together to make pools that overflow, and run like little rivers into other pools.

—Other families.

The connection is a feeling, that brings with it for Tim, the memory of Mischa playing in the rain.

The word father centres itself quietly. Mischa in a uniform, he'd never let it happen.

Mischa dies.

He punches the reset button. He can feel Vera watching him, standing in the doorway. It's her fault he forgot to read what the fairy said! He can feel her wanting to talk. He doesn't want to talk. Wishes she'd go away. Tild and Sweany start fighting in the kitchen. He thinks she'll go and sort things out. She doesn't. She wants to sort him out.

He turns around. Looks straight at her. Challenges her. Vera tries a smile. Mischa pushes her away with his eyes. She leaves him. In the kitchen someone knocks over a chair. He hears a slap. Tild screams. Some things can't be sorted. Mischa turns back to his game.

'Make him see reason!'

Vera is talking to her mother. She keeps thinking she is talking to Tim's mother.

—Make him see reason!

She can't say those things to Mischa. Make him believe his father's dead. Break him.

'Sorry Mum I have to go. Can't talk now.'

She doesn't wait to hear what her mother says. Maybe Tim is dead, maybe he isn't, she doesn't know. But Mischa thinks he knows and that's more than she has. Vera looks up. Joe has brought her a cup of tea.

'They haven't even got a body,' she says, and the tears won't stay back any more.

Tha Kin Maung arrives again just before dusk. Talks briefly with U Yewada and leaves quickly.

'Eat please,' says U Yewada, signalling for Tim to help himself. U Yewada takes food for Aik. He will not eat now. He is a monk. It is after midday.

Tim takes his food outside. Squats, his back against the mountain. Chews slowly. Not just because of stones. But because red rice is always hard in the centre, even though the grains are broken. Poor man's rice, thinks Tim.

—Nothing fluffy or white about it.

Inside the cave U Yewada is talking to Aik. His words have a rhythm. Slow and measured. Tim wonders what he's saying. What the Boy has told him. He cannot know. All he can know is what U Yewada tells him.

Tim turns his ear to listen to the breeze that is Burma. Tries to reconcile this Burma with the Burma of his seven-day visa, fifteen years ago. He hadn't seen any of this. No-one said anything. Everyone seemed happy.

Tim remembers trying to pocket a silver teaspoon from the Strand Hotel in Rangoon, a souvenir. The waiter politely asked him to return it. Counting cutlery was part of his job.

—He had to pay for what was stolen!

Tim finally gets it.

Flashes on the memory of a woman in Tazi as he got off the train, her baby, skin and bones, screaming.

—She had the eyes of a junkie.

—No, that's what they said.

Tim tries to think for himself.

—She had the eyes of someone without dreams.

—Not pretty.

—They got rid of her, quickly.

Tim remembers worrying about the baby. Catches the memory and wonders how he could have worried about the child without being concerned for the mother. The question is too big. Gives him a headache. He dams the thought.

'Everything in Burma is nice.'

He remembers the manager, at the hotel he stayed at, saying this.

—And I believed him.

Dusk drizzles into evening. Night swallows the valleys.

—Not completely.

The memory of the black garnet Buddha has surfaced. The cancer.

—It was easier to pretend.

The hairs on the back of Tim's arms rise.

He is seeing things through Vera's eyes. She would say he had set this whole situation up. Cause and effect. Fifteen years ago he had gone to Burma believing he would learn something. But he hadn't. He'd wanted a different lesson, one that fitted his view of things.

Tim feels slightly ill. Wonders if karma can work that quickly. Be drawn in such a tight circle. Vera thinks it can. He didn't think it could. But then there are so many different kinds of karma.

Tim thinks he smells smoke. Sniffs like an animal. Imagines villages burning.

'They're making coal.'

U Yewada is standing in the mouth of the cave.

'In the earth roots burn all night. In the morning they will be coal.'

Tim smiles. His heart is beating faster than it should be. His thoughts got away from him. He tries to think of something to say.

'Does it get cold here in winter?'

'A little.'

U Yewada suggests Tim come in now. Behind him a single candle flame illuminates the cave. Tim slaps at the mosquitoes around his ankles.

'Better we burn some incense,' says U Yewada.

Tim hadn't even thought about the mosquito. He used to be so careful not to harm insects.

—Always took lots of Rid.

It had been easy to be mindful with insect repellant.

It is an awkward moment, the first time Tim shakes Aik's hand. He feels he knows the Boy. He's held him. Dragged him. Arms chained around the slight cage that is his chest. And before that, the cell, the river! None of this, however, seems to Tim to be in the Boy. He even looks different, more like a child.

—Kindness can do that.

Tim is aware of U Yewada's hand resting gently on Aik's shoulder.

He tries smiling.

The Boy does not respond.

U Yewada speaks, filling in the distance between them.

'Aik would like to apologise for any pain and suffering

he has caused you. And asks please, that you do not take it personally.'

Tim feels the breath of his habit to 'laugh it off' rise. Stops himself.

'It's OK,' he says, and he means it.

U Yewada translates.

Aik looks down, averts his eyes. Tim realises the Boy is trying not to cry.

—Boys don't cry.

'There is one problem for Aik,' says U Yewada, 'He cannot stay here. It is not safe for him.'

'I know, that's why I said—'

U Yewada holds up one hand to silence Tim.

'But if he goes with you and you tell the Thai police he is one of the ones who took you, he will be arrested and killed. Here he will be killed. There he will be killed. It is very complicated.'

'Then we won't tell them.'

'You would do that?'

Tim pulls himself back from the brink of the impulse to acquiesce.

He has no intention of putting the Boy knowingly in more danger but there are things he wants to know, wants to understand before he agrees to anything. The Boy has given him nothing, no reason to trust.

'Maybe,' he says and lets the possibility settle.

'But I need to know more than I do now.'

Strategy can be instinctive.

U Yewada accepts Tim's request as reasonable. Explains to Aik. Tim is stung by the depth of the Boy's suspicion, the flash of his eyes.

U Yewada is quick to step in.

'You are a Buddhist,' he says. 'So you might know what I would tell Aik.'

Tim doesn't think he wants to say anything right at this moment.

'Without honesty there is no real growth and freedom. Aik is young. He has suffered greatly. In another life he might have done something really terrible to people.'

—What about this life?

Tim's eyes give him away. U Yewada answers his unspoken query.

'In Pali we call this *Wit*. Aik has done terrible things. But there are reasons. He will tell you. He has a good heart. If he is honest now, he does not have to carry that karma with him. He can go on from here. Have a good life.'

Tim nods. He understands Aik is just a boy. He tries to ease his face into a smile.

The Boy eyes him warily.

U Yewada's words reassure the Boy. Tim doesn't know their meaning, but he can read the tone. He works to keep his expression clear. His face open.

Finally the Boy nods agreement. Looks at Tim.

'OK,' he says.

Giving Tim the strange sounding word he knows is English.

'OK,' says Tim.

And he drags over his sleeping mat to sit cross-legged in front of the Boy. U Yewada pours them the last of the tea from Tha Kin Maung's thermos. The candle splutters. Outside water drips from the trees. Aik will not look at Tim. He watches U Yewada. Tim sits with the pulse of their difference.

'Why did you kidnap me?' is the first question Tim asks.

U Yewada translates.

Aik looks confused, answers with a single word as though he were being grilled.

Instead of translating, U Yewada speaks with Aik, says something that almost makes him smile. Not quite, but Tim sees the possibility.

Aik begins again. U Yewada leans towards him, encouraging him to find the words. When U Yewada translates he looks at Tim.

'They had orders to kidnap a Westerner from near the refugee camps. They stopped a bus two days before yours. But the tourist had got off. That is why they took you. They would have liked an American. They thought you were American.'

Tim can't hide his smile. What he suspects will become the single most important event of his life was a mistake.

'His Captain told him it was a clever plan to blame the kidnapping on the ethnic rebels in the camps and the Communists.'

The Boy is beginning to find the words.

'But it was very secret.'

U Yewada translates immediately. Sets up a rhythm between himself and the Boy, a phrase at a time.

'No-one was allowed to say anything or they would be shot.

'There were only six of them chosen by the Captain for this mission.

'He was very scared.

'His Captain said this was his chance to become an officer.

'He did not really believe him. Only Burmen are officers. Never ethnics.

'But he thought maybe if he was an officer it would be better.

'He would not do what other officers did.'

Tim looks at the Boy. Behind the mask of his face, Tim sees deep gouges in the wood of him, they surface in his eyes.

'Why, what did the other officers do?' Tim has to ask. U Yewada translates the question.

The Boy eyes Tim. He is on the other side of a gorge uncertain of the bridge between them. He sanitises his response into a single statement.

'Many officers are very cruel,' translates U Yewada.

'Yes they are.'

Tim feels the rod of his father. His words are touched with the memory, he didn't mean to say that. The Boy catches his sentiment, opens a little.

'They take everything for themselves. From the soldiers, from the people.

'They tell you as a soldier you will get food and medicine. But the officers sell it on the black market.

'We are told to buy what we need. But we never get paid. So we cannot.

'If a soldier says anything he is punished, beaten.'

Now Aik has started he can't stop.

'Once I told my Captain "You're wrong!" Then he said, "Why did you say that?" and hit and kicked me.

'I thought being a soldier would be better than being a porter.'

The Boy is crossing the bridge between himself and Tim, a statement at a time.

'I did not know what to do.

'I do not have any family.

'As an orphan you are nothing, without prospect.

'I hate the soldiers. That they did that to me.

'They killed my father. His name was Wana.

'I never met him. I saw a photo once.

'Then they killed my mother.'

Red stings the Boy's eyes. A lapse of control, Tim feels the choking of another's heart.

'They took us from our village.

'Made us work long hours crushing rocks to make roads.

'Always the soldiers are taking people.

'There is nothing you can do.

'One day some rocks fell on my mother.

'She was very badly injured. They just left her. There was no medicine.

'But she would not die. So they shot her.

'After that they took me as a porter.'

The Boy's statements come like gunfire. U Yewada struggles to keep pace.

'Being a porter was bad.

'They made us carry very heavy loads. There was no food.

'If you cried they hit you. We had no rights.

'We were scared.

'We had to walk in front of the soldiers in case there were mines.

'At Ho Paung there were three hundred porters and five hundred prisoners at the front-line.

'At the end of the fighting there were only twenty porters left.'

Ghosts see through the Boy's eyes.

'My Captain said I was lucky.'

The Boy's face is beginning to crack. There is the pressure of truth.

'He gave me a gun.

'Made me shoot two porters who were injured.

'I did not want to do it.'

Truth shatters the Boy's mask. Tears run in rivers down his face.

'But if I did not kill them, I would be killed myself.'

Aik is a child. He is ashamed. He hangs his head. His last words, small, sit on a ledge of rock in the cave. U Yewada translates.

'He thought it would be better if he was one of them.'

Tim watches the splash of the Boy's tears on the back of his hand.

—The last rain.

It's just a thought.

Inside the slow combustion of anger is overtaking Tim. There is heat in his chest, that makes him think of peat and bogs and burning.

'I have to tell them it was the army who kidnapped me,' he says.

'But not about Aik?' U Yewada is quick to clarify.

'No,' says Tim, 'But I want names. His Captain's name. And the names of the men who gave the order.'

The words are out before Tim's thought about what they mean. What he's planning.

U Yewada does not smile. But his eyes dance. He explains to the boy what Tim has asked. Tim watches Aik, head bent, wonders what Aik thinks of all this. Suddenly Aik looks up straight into Tim's face.

'*Kyay-zue tin bar dae*,' he says.

Words too gentle for such a fierce face.

'He says thank you,' explains U Yewada.
Inside Tim, feeling tumbles like coarse sand.

'No problem,' he says.
Caught in the rip of the tide.

Tim cannot even pronounce the name of Aik's Captain, let alone the names of the other officers at the central headquarters who gave the order. U Yewada writes them down.

Tim looks at the list. Has the strangest sense about the writing. The marks on the page identify men he's never met, single them out from millions, like a strange kind of sorcery. The Boy could not write the list. He knows. But he could not write the list. U Yewada's words come back to Tim. 'Thieves can steal all treasures but education.'

The Boy asks something. Tim looks up.

'He wants to know if you're going to fight them?' says U Yewada.
Tim is slow to answer. Cautious of making promises he can't keep.

'Maybe,' he says.
He has clear intention, litigation.

—Fuck the bastards!
He's going to pull the righteous bastards from their ivory towers.

—It's wrong.

—What's happened to the Boy is wrong.

—What's happening in Burma is wrong.
After only a few weeks his body is so wrecked he can feel his own mortality. His stomach crawls with aberrant cramps from hunger and bacteria. His shoulders have been wrenched, torn, so he can feel the gap between ball and socket where the damp gets in, turns cold and sits. There

is always a line of pain across his skull from the crack of the rifle. He remembers how you see a flash in the black of the eyes shutting when the head is hit. Wonders how many times the Boy's head has been hit.

—Fuck them all.

He wants to kill someone.

Tim catches a glimpse of the Boy's exhaustion in the guttering light of the cheap candle and is caught between the impulse to stroke his head as a father, or clasp his hand as a friend. Instead he touches Aik's shoulder as he stands. The tenderness is in the awkward nature of the gesture.

'Good night,' he says, 'I hope tomorrow you feel better.'

U Yewada translates. Tim leaves the cave.

In the empty dark tears come, anger, hurt.

—How can people do this?

—Create hell on earth?

Tim breathes in, compresses his anger. The air is rich, fecund, growing. His mind grabs the scent.

—Where there should be paradise.

The contradiction fuels his intent.

Tim imagines international courts. He is placing his faith in the justice of law. A voice in his head warns this is pretty shaky ground. He doesn't even know if it's possible. He'll think about that later. Right now he has to believe it is. Otherwise the corruption will just go on and on. He's not ready to accept that's the way things work.

Tim takes all the pain from his body, knots his muscles with tension. He can feel the heat of anger boiling his blood, the enormity of the injustice. If it takes his whole life he's going to bring those bastards down. He has to. He can't live with doing nothing. But they have to get out first.

Tim begins to worry about how long they'll have to wait before they can leave. How long it'll be before Aik is strong. He wonders how far the border is. How long it'll take them to get through. Wonders about the enemy.

—Patrols.

How will they know? How will they get around them? He tries to calm himself, tells himself there's no point worrying now, that he should just sleep and ask U Yewada in the morning. Then he can worry.

—But what if Aik doesn't get better?

—What if he's never strong enough to walk out?

—We'll make him a stretcher!

—Carry him!

—The old men can't carry him.

—Drag him!

—I can drag him on a stretcher.

Tim's mind just won't let go. Now he's worrying about what kind of wood to use for the stretcher.

—Something green.

—Supple to give suspension.

He breathes out, tries to let some of the tension go.

The moon moves out from behind the clouds, cuts into the open sky of the west. Its clean beauty makes him want to cry. He's missing Mischa. Hopes Mischa doesn't think he's dead. Doesn't want to put him through that. Doesn't want to put scars in his clear eyes.

Tim bounces his love off the moon before he even realises what he's doing. It's the same moon.

Lying in bed, Mischa knows she'll come.

It's the first time he can remember not wanting her to tuck him in. He hears her coming. Pretends he's asleep. She comes in anyway. Sits on the edge of his bed. Strokes the hair back off his face.

He opens his eyes. They look at each other. She smiles. He can see the words building in her. Any moment she's going to start talking. He shuts down. Wishes she'd get on with it so he could go to sleep. It doesn't matter what she says, he's not going to believe his Dad's dead.

'There are things we're going to have to do Mischa,' Vera says quietly. 'There'll be a service I guess.'

Mischa feels himself burrow deeper into the iron of his will.

—Here she goes!

In the next room Sweany starts throwing toys, shaking the side of his cot, singing out.

'No. No. No. No!'

Vera leaves Sweany to Joe.

'I'm getting old Mischa,' she says. 'I don't know things the way I used to, from the inside out.'

Mischa sees the grey in his mother's hair, the lines on her face. He doesn't usually notice them.

'That's the truly horrible part of growing up,' she says. 'You become grounded and your feet get heavy and you stop listening to angels. I always thought I'd know if anything happened to Tim. I've always known with him and I didn't feel anything. But I don't trust that any more. I believe what I'm told now. But that doesn't mean it's right and you're wrong. It's just that I'm getting old.'

Mischa feels all the fight go out of him. Vera smiles to ward off the tears.

''Night,' she says. 'You know where I am if you need me.'

She stands then.

Mischa catches her at the door.

'I love you Mum.'

Her eyes are tired.

'Love you too.'

Leaving Burma.

Aik never thought he would. He wonders how it will be with the other refugees. He is Wa, not Burmen. But he has fought for the SLORC. He thinks perhaps one night someone will kill him anyway, even if they make it across the border to a camp.

Lying on his side, looking out into the dark, Aik realises he has been expecting to die for a long time. He remembers that his father was a scholar. And wonders what it would be to read a book.

His eyes are drawn to the silhouette of Tim, sitting hunched, outside the cave.

—Tired. Really tired.

When he was very young he had believed someone would save him. A good man, a Captain maybe, would say, 'Stop! This is not right.' It never happened.

Aik closes his eyes. He's not thinking any more.

Outside, Tim is lost in the darkness thinking of Mischa. The chorus from an old song going round in his head.

—'We'll get together then son. You know we'll have a good time then.'

Vera gave him a tape of that song once.

'Listen to it,' she said. 'And I mean listen to it.'

Mischa was four. Tim didn't listen to it. He knew the words.

—'When you coming home Dad? I don't know when.' Vera put nails on her boots when she made a point. Left him nowhere to go. Underlined his faults until that's all there was. Then he couldn't change, not without losing ground. Missing hurts.

—'We'll get together then, Dad. You know we'll have a good time then.'

Missing really hurts.

Tim finally gets it. Sitting in the middle of the Burmese jungle, smoke up his nostrils, nowhere to go, he finally gets it. This was always going to happen. One day when he was old and it was too late he'd be sitting there missing his son. Hurting. And Vera knew.

—'We'll get together then, Dad. You know we'll have a good time then.'

—Was trying to warn me.

Tim thinks about Vera.

The way she lives her life from the inside out, feeling. Swimming the length of underground rivers, trying to navigate. Be prepared for what's coming up ahead. He's never seen the point. Realises he's a surface dweller.

Tim never wanted to see himself that way. But he is. Always there are things he has to do. Distractions. Loose commitments. That let him skim across the surface of situations. Take what he likes. Not delve too deep. Now there are none, and missing hurts. And he understands.

—She was looking out for me.

—Looking up ahead.

Tim always thought it was only Mischa she cared about.

Tenderness replaces anger. Inside something gives. He doesn't have to fight her any more. He wishes he'd never told her he only stayed because of Mischa. It wasn't true.

Tim breathes out, lets it go.

—Can't change the past.

—Only the future.

When he gets home, he's going to take Mischa to the beach.

Monkeys start. Fight among themselves and then fall quiet. A moment of discord and then it's over.

—And there is only the future.

—Clean.

—Uncluttered.

Tim's never had that feeling before. Which doesn't make sense since there was always a future. Only when he looks back at how he used to see the future, the feeling inside is of a sort of nothing. Just more of the same. When he thinks of the future now, inside there is a feeling of expanse. A certainty that it will somehow make sense of all the fractured pieces of the past.

His mother, his father, Vera, Mischa, his art, Nepal, Rimpoche, are all streaming through the eye of a needle, which is now. The moment bridging past and future.

Tim isn't scared any more. Can't explain why. Can only understand it himself as a feeling in his body. A certain wholeness. As though he's fitted the right peg to the hole inside. If he follows that feeling he knows everything will be alright. Even if it means he's got to do some stuff he doesn't want to do at the time.

—In the end it will be right.

Tim wonders how long he's been fighting that knowledge.

—Quite a while.

—Years.

He's growing up. The sensation is quite strange at forty-odd. This is what he was meant to do in his twenties.

—But you don't do you.

—Give it up unless you have to.

Childhood is what Tim is thinking about. His mind goes to the Boy.

—No childhood at all.

For the first time in Tim's life he feels truly lucky. Has the strangest sense that there is a lot he's taken for granted.

Tiredness overcomes him. He has to sleep now. Thinks about sleeping outside. He feels safer outside. It's inside he feels trapped. Inside, there's nowhere to run. He tells himself at home it will be different. Goes back inside the cave. Lies on his right side, one hand under his head like the reclining Buddha.

Aik cries out in his sleep. A nightmare. Images fill Tim's mind. Imaginings of the Boy's dreams. He is fighting injustice in his sleep. He never wins. It's just bad, really bad. U Yewada begins to chant. Aik quietens. Fingers of mist reach out, damp, into the cool of the night.

Tim seduces his mind towards sleep with meditation. Realises how much strength it takes to fight a war with non-violence.

—You have to be smart.

—Smarter than the enemy.

—Compassion.

The word settles him.

—Without compassion, there is only revenge.

As sleep pulls Tim under, he glimpses a world where the mess of the past isn't pulled with the thread through the eye of the needle, but left behind.

—Can't be changed.

—There's only the future.

Bob phones in the early evening.

'Mr Rhyder, I just thought you should know. We've heard from the Australian envoys who flew into the BCMC camp today. I'm afraid the trip didn't clarify anything.'

'How unexpected,' the thought slips out.

'Mr Rhyder, I really can assure you we are looking into every possibility.'

'Yes. I'm sure you are,' says the Captain. 'Thank you Bob. For letting us know.'

The Captain hangs up the phone. Feels totally alone. No-one knows what happened to his son. No-one wants to know.

—Too dangerous.

—In warfare there are no constant conditions.

Thoughts go round and round in the Captain's head.

—The wise Captain understands the concerns of all parties involved.

Only he and his wife are concerned about their son.

Just before dawn, as Tim's consciousness rises, he dreams. He takes the Boy home to his family. The Captain doesn't know the Boy's a Gook.

—Of course he's blind!

Tim had forgotten.

The Captain shakes the Boy's dark hand.

—It's all alright.

His mother fusses, there are lamingtons and a white tablecloth with apricot flowers. Tim realises he is a boy again. In his parents' house he is always sixteen. He suddenly remembers Mischa. He's left him at the airport. He wishes he'd stop doing that, leaving him behind. He tells his mother he has to go back.

'Go back to the airport and get Mischa.'

She doesn't know what he's talking about. He is only sixteen. There is no Mischa.

Tim wakes feeling like shit, his bones hurt. He wraps his blanket around himself and goes outside. The sun is rising, opaque through cloud, choked. Today there is no horizon.

—No Shangri-la.

Tim takes it as an omen.

'Been in Asia too long, that's my problem.'

He goes to find a hidden place and shit.

When he comes back, U Yewada and Aik are awake. The Boy is stronger. He is up. Squatting outside the cave warming his hands on a small fire he tends, while U Yewada steeps herbs in the old tin can. A tea for the Boy.

'Morning,' says Tim, trying out cheerful.

Aik's eyes lock on him for an instant, fierce. Then he drops his gaze and goes back to tending the fire.

'Is he alright?' asks Tim.

'He is Wa. Wa take their dreams very seriously. Last night he had bad dreams. Says today will not be good.'

Tim smiles at the coincidence of omens. Drops the pretence of cheerfulness.

—Some days are just not cheery.

By mid morning however, when Tha Kin Maung has still not come, and the clouds have not cleared but rather churn with heat like a Swedish sauna, and Tim's stomach growls, Tim finds himself looking at the coincidence of omens more as premonition.

—Not that it changes anything.

—It's still not a good day.

He paces outside the cave, U Yewada has asked him not to wander far. Says Tha Kin Maung would have come if he could. That something must be wrong. Aik thinks perhaps the SLORC have come. Tim's sure they've come for him. U Yewada says they could have come for many reasons. Tim is not convinced. Fear constricts his heart. He wants to get out of this fucking country. He's scared soon he will fear his own shadow.

—Just because you're paranoid doesn't mean they're not out to get you.

The old saying comes to mind and it's not funny.

Breathe, Tim tells himself, breathe. And he tries to let the fear go, squeeze it out with his breath. It doesn't help.

The rain comes early, just after noon, a torrential downpour that lasts four hours. Tim squats in the mouth of the cave, feels like a fish in a bowl. Outside the world has turned to water. Only in the bowl is there air. He watches the war in the sky, flashes of lightning and thunder.

Tha Kin Maung arrives in the middle of the afternoon, sheltered under his broken red umbrella. He brings three packages of rice wrapped in banana leaves. He says the SLORC have come. Are in his village. Says he cannot stay, that they should leave as soon as it is dark.

Before he goes, Tha Kin Maung clasps Tim's hand.

'Buddha,' he says.

Kindness floats in his old eyes.

'Buddha,' says Tim.

Tha Kin Maung smiles.

Tim watches the old man disappear into the jungle. Bare feet, beneath a red umbrella.

When he is gone Tim suggests they leave as soon as the rain begins to ease. U Yewada explains it is not safe. There are sentries. They would be seen.

'We must walk only at night,' he says.

Aik's brow is furrowed when he speaks.

Tim doesn't understand the words but he can tell something's worrying him.

—Of course something's worrying him.

Tim's mind flicks through the options.

—The SLORC!

—Getting to the border!

—The Thai police!

U Yewada rubs his pa-di between the palms of his hands, prays a little before he answers.

Aik accepts what U Yewada says. Although he does not seem convinced. U Yewada pats Aik on the shoulder, smiles. Tells him to eat. Aik begins to open his package of rice.

'You also! Eat! Eat!' says U Yewada to Tim.

Slowly, Tim does the same. U Yewada will not eat until the next morning.

'A problem?' asks Tim.

U Yewada looks for the right words.

'Aik is frightened of the jungle at night,' he says.

Tim thinks of mines, his father's lost sight.

'Why? What's the problem?'

Tim's stomach picks up the scent of rice, growls.

'*Om ah hung*,' he dedicates the food under his breath.

—Body, speech and mind.

Begins to eat. Aware that this food, he is offering mostly to his body. Despite his hunger he makes himself chew carefully. Would rather avoid a cracked tooth.

'Many people,' says U Yewada, 'are scared of the jungle at night. Of spirits and ghosts.'

This is not what Tim was expecting.

He looks at Aik eating, silent, serious. The set of his brow fierce despite his youth. Remembers what he's been through, and finds it strange to think him frightened of ghosts. Says so.

U Yewada snaps, his gaze pins Tim.

'The boy has done bad things. It is not wrong to be careful.'

Rice sticks in the back of Tim's throat.

'No. I didn't mean—'

He can't finish the sentence, doesn't know what it is he didn't mean, just that he didn't mean whatever it is U Yewada heard in his words. He was just thinking out loud. His sincerity disarms the strung bow in U Yewada's eyes.

'In your country, when people see things, have problems in their minds, what happens to them?' asks U Yewada.

Tim knows he's hit a nerve. This is personal for U Yewada.

'They get analysed,' Tim says, 'sedated. Some get locked up.'

U Yewada nods. He knows.

'Very hard,' he says. 'Very hard.'

Sitting in the mouth of a cave, rain stamping down the heat of the afternoon, it does seem that way to Tim; very hard.

—Unnecessary.

'There are I think better ways,' says U Yewada. 'Older cultures allow more room for the unseen.'

Tim has never looked at belief in terms of the breadth of psychological cohesion of a culture before. His brain registers the thought as sensation, the memory of a sherbet bomb.

—Smart.

He thinks.

—U Yewada is very smart.

The idea makes sense.

He had a friend once, said ghosts were driving her crazy. No-one believed her. Everyone knew it was the acid. They locked her up. She was dead now.

—But if someone had believed her?

Tim has a sense that kindness might have helped more than diagnosis. The parameters of his own culture seem suddenly very narrow. Heavy, black parallel lines that squeeze in upon the space between them, leaving only a trace of light, a thin white line.

—Charcoal on white.

He stores the image.

Tim can't help but guess at why U Yewada feels so strongly about this.

—A mother?

—A lover?

—A sister?

He notices how he thinks it must have been a woman.

—Could have been a brother.

He'd love to ask. Can't.

—Not without a few beers.

It occurs to Tim that perhaps U Yewada does not believe in ghosts, only in mental health. The thought unnerves him. Even he believes in ghosts.

—Not that I've ever seen one.

Always there is the voice in him that keeps the back door

open. Doesn't want to get caught out believing the wrong thing because he hasn't thought it through.

—A Jesuit education.

He thinks.

—A questioning mind.

Still he likes that voice, it grounds him.

'You don't believe in spirits, Ka Daw?' he asks.

'Of course I believe in spirits. I am Burmese!'

Tim almost laughs.

—How could he not!

'And I am Buddhist!'

U Yewada's eyes share the joke with Tim.

Tim laughs.

'All those offerings to hungry ghosts would be hard if you didn't believe.'

In his mind he offers the last mouthful of rice. His fingers leave only a grain.

U Yewada runs the beads of his pa-di through his hand. An almost imperceptible movement.

'Spirits are part of life,' he says.

And in the west the sun breaks through. Tim watches rays of gold set the green to dancing.

—Slipping.

He thinks.

—From shadow to light.

And smiles at his own tendency to become poetic over the last flush of a dying day. When his stomach still growls, and the boy he is travelling with carries his own sunset, the flush of fever.

'Beautiful isn't it?' says U Yewada.

'Yes,' says Tim.

It is and he wants to go home.

'How long till we get to the border?' he asks.

'Six days maybe.'

'Are you coming to Thailand?'

'No,' says U Yewada. 'When we get closer, Aik can find the way.'

'Where did you learn to speak English?'

Tim senses he may not get another opportunity to ask.

Seventy years of Burma's history touches Tim in U Yewada's words. He tastes the changes, from Raj, to Independence, to the corruption of a dream, in the way he says, 'Oxford, I grew up there', and 'It was very cold.'

Mischa is OK.

All day he is OK. Feels sort of normal. Vera seems better too. Stronger. It's even OK when other people come, bringing soup and their own grief. Vera makes them tea. Her eye catching Mischa's as he disappears with a handful of biscuits to another room.

It doesn't matter what people say. He can believe what he likes. His Mum doesn't think he's crazy. Mischa knows he didn't understand all of what she said. But he understood that much. He thinks maybe not listening to angels is like not stopping to read what the fairy had to say.

When Tim comes home they will go to the beach. When Mischa thinks like this he is certain.

They leave just before nightfall.

Cotton blankets wrapped around them like shawls. It gets dark quickly as they descend into the jungle. No-one talks. They strain to see, to not lose their footing. The jungle's steep. The smell of humus rises strong with every step, almost intoxicating. Their feet disturb the jungle debris, open the seal of its litter.

—Secrets.

Thinks Tim.

—The world will be alright when there are no more secrets.

—When the skin is peeled back.

He shudders at the graphic image of his own thought. Jesus, he wishes they had a torch. Were out of here. Gone. That it was over.

Slowly his eyes adjust and his brain stops questioning what he can't see. U Yewada moves through the jungle almost soundlessly. Aik, close on his heels, is agile, light. Tim feels himself the weighted klutz bringing up the rear. He slips and slides, vine tangles his feet, trees dump their collected water with his passing. Suddenly U Yewada stops. There is the rhythmic pounding of stone and grain.

'SLORC,' whispers Aik.

The light of the rising moon catches in Aik's eye. Plays theatre with his face. Tim sees the dance between fear and hate. His heart beats fast. The scent of coal is in the air.

'Soldiers hull rice at night,' whispers U Yewada. 'Villagers do not hull rice at night.'

Tim understands they are near Tha Kin Maung's village.

—Must be careful.

They move off.

Tim tries to keep his step light. His breathing even. His heart where it should be, in his chest. He reaches out to steady himself, his palms are sweating. He can't imagine living like this all the time, always scared.

The luck of their rescue suddenly strikes him. He didn't stop and think, didn't look around before he dragged Aik out into the open. Didn't even see Tha Kin Maung until he was standing over them. Tha Kin Maung could just as easily have been a soldier as a farmer.

—Not cut out for this.

Yet even as Tim thinks the words he can feel himself learning. He is listening harder. Breathing quieter. Is becoming suspicious, even of the quiet, as they descend into the next valley. Tim doesn't like that change. Part of him is getting a taste for the game and that frightens him almost more than the enemy. He thinks of his father.

—What would he do if there was no-one to fight?

—What will he do without me?

They cross a small stream running between rocks. Already it is beginning to swell with monsoon rain. Tim hadn't thought about that. Wonders what it will mean for them, swollen rivers. Aik takes a drink.

—At least we won't go thirsty.

Tim does the same. The water is cool and mineral strong, alive in his mouth. U Yewada asks if they would like to rest.

—No!

Tim catches the word in his throat. Lets Aik answer.

—Maybe he needs to rest.

'*Hint-inn, ma-yut phu.*'

Aik definitely does not want to rest. Tim smiles to himself, he had forgotten about the spirits.

Through the night they rest only when they have to, mostly after hard climbs, and then only until their bodies begin to cool and they can keep walking. U Yewada keeps to the more densely wooded tracks of jungle, avoiding where possible the open scars of logging. In the moonlight these scars seem to Tim like deserted battlefields. They disturb him.

'Soldiers have to make money,' whispers U Yewada.

'They don't think much about anything else.'

U Yewada's explanation allows Tim to understand. It's not the logging. He's seen logging scars before. It's the way the logging has been done. Without regard. Everything that was in the way has been flattened. That's how things are done in Burma. And he and Aik are in the way. In someone's way.

In the dark, the severing of bone and sinew, of warm blood feeding earth, seems a real possibility. Tim feels the pall of horror threaten rational sense. Shuts his mind down. Concentrates on walking. His feet are going to walk him out of here.

'Om mani padme hum, om mani padme hum . . .'

Tim recites the mantra. Lets it rumble in his chest. The vibration helps. Stops him thinking.

To their right, somewhere lost in the dark, there is movement. Tim drops, ready to fight. Aik picks up a stick and beats the jungle.

'*Thwar! Thwar!*'

Tim catches a glimpse of yellowed tusks and dark smudged rumps retreating.

—Wild boar.

And he was ready, even for spirits.

Long before dawn Tim senses the sun rise, notices the shifting weight of night. His right leg shakes as though he has the palsy when they climb. He is exhausted. What he'd give for a cup of hot tea with sugar, eggs on toast.

—Home.

He can taste it, smell it.

—Soon.

He's going home.

U Yewada stops at the edge of the jungle. Ahead mist rises from rough ploughed fields, laps at a handful of stilted bamboo houses, where chained dogs bark.

'We will stay here,' says U Yewada.

Aik shakes his head. The Boy's doubt triggers Tim's.

'You sure it's safe?'

The question springs from his gut.

'There are no soldiers here,' says U Yewada, stepping out into the open.

'Aik is Wa. They are the traditional poppy growers. He is suspicious of the Lahu. They are their main competitors, that is all. But the Lahu are fierce enemies of the Burmese Army.'

Tim's eyes take in the tightly woven fences of bamboo stakes around the perimeter of the village, the barbed wire.

'They grow poppies?'

U Yewada nods.

'We will be safe here.'

It's then Tim sees the trenches.

Walking across the open rough ploughed fields Tim takes in the clear vantage of the small village's position. There is no way to approach the village without being seen. It is impenetrable to all but air attack. He thinks of the planes that bombed their camp. The ones U Yewada said were American gifts to fight the Opium War, and once again he is left to think that things in Burma are rarely what they seem.

As they enter the village Tim notices the lean poverty of the chickens and is struck by the thought that growing drugs doesn't pay much.

At the headman's house they are welcomed. The headman is very interested in their story. Tim wonders how much of their story U Yewada is telling him. Enough of the truth, he thinks, that Aik should seem embarrassed by the old Lahu man's acceptance; a slap on the back and fighting words. Despite himself, Aik seems to stand a little taller. Tim's eyes keep drifting to the chained monkey under the headman's stilted house. He is too tired.

Inside they are given a bowl of thin sticky rice and tea and a place to sleep. Tim takes it all in like a series of photos, snapshots to be processed later. He will remember the young girl who serves them rice, by the curve of her neck, framed in black, her hair, and the brightly woven edge of her clothing. Aik, he notices, has begun to sweat a little. And perhaps his hands shake. Tim is worried. But he has to lie down. He hopes Aik will be alright. Sleep takes Tim as easily as heat takes the day.

Free.

Lying on his side Aik tries to imagine what that will be like. Out of the corner of his eye he watches the women of the house. The headman did not hold it against him that he had been a soldier. He seemed to understand. Had even given him rice. Maybe things would be alright. Watching the women Aik thinks one day he would like a family.

He looks at the shaggy white guy, already sleeping. He looked better when they took him off the bus. Aik remembers he didn't like him then. He does now. He thinks he is a good man. When he was young Aik thought most men were good. He doesn't any more. He remembers his mother saying his father was a good man. Died for them. For the hope of a better future.

—He was a scholar.

—He died a warrior.

The old story plays itself out, pictures in Aik's mind, as he is pulled into sleep.

It's hard being the keeper.

The stronger Vera grows the weaker Mischa becomes. The looks she needs from him when they watch the news. The way she takes his hand, squeezes it. Puts him between her and the world, wears him down. Until he's not certain any more.

They show his Dad's picture on the news.

'It doesn't look like him,' says Mischa.

And his heart begins to beat so fast he thinks he will be sick. He doesn't know what he believes any more.

Mischa wakes, at two forty-five a.m., gasping for air. He is having an asthma attack. He has never had one before. Vera makes him breathe into a paper bag. It doesn't help. His lips and his eyelids are blue. The tips of his fingers. He can see that. Joe calls an ambulance. When they arrive they help him to breathe. Put a mask over his face and help him to breathe.

The night is dark. The lights in the ambulance are bright, like stickers. Vera is with him. Being in the hospital makes him feel better. There is nothing there, only sterile things. He is given something to make him sleep. He is allowed to spend the night.

When he wakes Vera is beside him, asleep in a chair. She looks soft and crumpled. She opens her eyes.

'Hi. How are you?'

Mischa had forgotten why they were here.

'OK I think,' he says.

He's breathing better now.

'Hard isn't it?' says Vera.

Mischa's not sure which hard she's talking about.

'Believing,' she says.

He feels tears hot in his eyes. Nods. Vera holds his hand and squeezes it. Doesn't try to take away his pain. It's better that way.

Tim's eyes seek out Aik as soon as he wakes.

He's there. Sitting up. Eating. His back against the wall.

—Alright. He's alright.

Tim hadn't meant to sleep. Somewhere he'd meant to do something. But his body had been so tired. Sitting up he notices it is almost dark. He's slept nearly the whole day. He is given a bowl of rice, a little turnip, and an egg. A special meal. And he is grateful.

As they leave Tim glimpses the headman relaxing back into an armchair under his house, opium pipe in hand. Nearby, bare-bottomed children play with stones.

U Yewada leads them along a narrow gorge that cuts through the opposing mountains. Tim struggles with the track, slipping in the mud, and on the rocks glistening wet. Ahead of him Aik moves nimble across the rugged terrain, and U Yewada's passage is so smooth, he seems to Tim an apparition. His ochre robes catching shadow, his silver hair catching light.

—What a story to tell Mischa.

Tim feels a brush of excitement, and the lightness helps with the terrain.

The gorge opens into a narrow valley, complete with stream, the run-off from a mass of ravines. They stop to catch their breath. Take a drink. Tim notices how silence can have density.

Aik comes and squats between Tim and U Yewada.

'*Kya-naw ah-phe har di-sit-tat ko taw-hlan pyi ah-thet sone khe ya tae so dar thu-go pyaw pya pay bar*,' he says, looking at Tim.

In the moonlight there is a knife edge in the whites of Aik's eyes.

'He wants you to know that his father died fighting the Burmese Army. He was executed because he would not agree,' says U Yewada.

'*Ah-khu kya-naw lut-lat pyi. Ah-phe tu thar phit aung jo-zar mae. Thu-loh ah-thet-pay yin pay ya pa zae.*'

'Aik says that now he is a free man, he will do the same. Even die if he has to.'

Tim doesn't know what to say. He can't tell the Boy not to fight.

—Of course he should fight.

—I'd fight.

—Something's not right.

Tim's mind is scrambling for answers.

—'Go into battle expecting to lose and you will.'

His father's words.

'Perhaps it would be better to fight and live,' says Tim looking at Aik.

U Yewada translates.

'*Ah-thet za-dae ya dar htet shin-tan taw-hlan ya dar po ah-date-pae shi mae htin dae.*'

Aik's brow furrows with thought.

'*Kya-naw jo-zar hma bar*,' he says.

U Yewada seems satisfied.

'He says he will think about that.'

The track U Yewada follows leads them down a steep ravine, where the earth has been churned by heavy pack animals, and finally into the foothills. Still mountains, by Tim's reckoning. Yet far more peopled. Tracks and paths criss-cross the jungle. Villages dot the ridges and valleys.

'Shan,' says U Yewada.

Pointing to one village perched just below the opposite ridge.

'Lishaw,' he says.

As they skirt around the outlying fields of another.

'Ankar, Pa-daung.'

The list goes on. Tim had not realised there were so many different people in Burma.

U Yewada leads them through a jungle tunnel and into the dense hinterland of the foothills. The track takes them to the open fields of a small village before cutting back into the jungle. The village leaves Tim with the strangest sense of desolation. He wonders why U Yewada didn't name the people who live there.

After a rough climb and a rugged descent that tests Tim's sense of hope and humour, they come to a village where nothing has been left standing. The houses have been burnt, the people chased away. U Yewada has brought them here because of the well. As Tim takes in the devastation violent hatred wells in him, and brings with it the taste of rotting. He rinses his mouth out and spits.

—Jesus I hate this fucking country.

He expels the thought on a breath.

'Centralisation,' says U Yewada, 'The Burmese Army has an effective policy. If there is resistance, they simply wipe out a village. They find it encourages others.'

Tim holds the weight of his head in his hands, thinks about the last village they passed.

—No life.

—That was it.

The sense of desolation.

Tim lifts his head. He has reached a point of saturation, the more he learns, the worse the nightmare becomes.

'Everything in Burma has been broken,' he says.

U Yewada draws water from the well. Hands him the rusted tin.

'We are alive,' he says, and smiles.

And Tim does think that's something.

An hour before sunrise they come to a Shan village where U Yewada says his cousin lives. This is where they will rest. Tim notices the stilted houses of the Shan are more delicate than Lahu houses.

Inside, he notices the weave of the bamboo walls and the glistening slate of the Boy's pallor. U Yewada assures Tim that after sleep and food Aik will be alright. Lying down to sleep, Tim feels the palpitations of his heart.

—Anxious.

He names the feeling.

—That something will go wrong.

He looks at Aik, curled like a child to sleep, and closes his own eyes. The day is something best slept through. He dreams himself violet.

Vera forgets why she came into the bathroom.

She is remembering another bathroom, another time. Ever since she heard the news. Ever since John phoned. She has been living back in that other time, when the organs of her body quivered with loving Tim.

She remembers taking the first step away from him. Leaving quietly through the back door without fuss. She knew there was another woman. A girl really. He sat next to her in his Tibetan class. They held hands. The infidelity of the heart could be crueller than the infidelity of the dick. It left her nowhere to go because Tim had actually done nothing.

—He was good at that.

She thinks.

—Doing nothing.

That's why it had been so easy for her to slip away. Leave him sitting in what he believed their relationship to be and not even notice she was gone, until she actually left.

Leaving Tim. Vera lets herself remember the day, standing in line to claim the sole supporting parent benefit from Social Security, she simply took off the rose-coloured glasses. Tim was home asleep in bed. He had a job. She shouldn't have been there. But he was saving to go to India. Didn't have to pay rent. She was in her mother's house then, that's why he was with her. He wasn't her partner.

Vera remembers how much it hurt seeing and accepting this. Accepting that she would always be standing alone in a line for sole parents because that's really how it was. And so she left him.

Vera makes herself breathe. She has never told anyone this. Not even Joe. She is ashamed because she was complicit. She never stood her ground and said, no, this is not good enough. Having a family, having me, isn't an optional extra. I'm not covering for you any more. She never said this because she didn't want to lose him, and so she tried filleting her heart instead. But in the end the practical pressures, the rent, the food, the childcare. Dealing with those things on her own put such a wedge between them, that liking each other and having the odd good time just wasn't enough.

Vera makes herself breathe. Love, she has come to believe is quite a practical thing. A slow-grown trust built over time.

She thinks of Joe. Loving him doesn't hurt.

'Mum! Is the bath ready?'

Tild has a voice like a foghorn. Quickly Vera turns on the taps, puts the plug in.

'Nearly!'

She gets two face washers from the cupboard, the bubble bath.

'Oh God I hope he's not dead.'

Nothing else matters any more.

For two days the Captain's wife does not get out of bed. Does not eat. Does not speak. The doctor prescribes anti-depressants. The Captain turns the bottle of pills in his hand, runs his thumb around the corrugated sides of its top.

'The doctor left some pills,' he says.

Joan keeps her eyes shut tight. Closes her ears against him until all she can hear is the sound of her own blood.

'He thought they might help.'

The Captain puts the pills on the table beside the bed.

Joan tries to tell herself it's not his fault. The thought lacks conviction. Love has turned to hate. Hate is her casing for grief. Without it she cannot breathe. Her heart is rotting, seeping black, into her blood.

The Captain sits. Perches on the end of the bed.

Every cell within Joan wants to hurt him. All she can do is hold herself tight. Not speak. Not move. Lock herself down. She can see herself cutting him into small pieces with a kitchen knife.

'Joan I don't know what to do,' he says.

His words land awkward on the bed between them. He's holding out a hand. In her mind she chops it off.

Outside, the next door neighbour's children play. Boy's voices, marks across the day that make her think of Tim. A strangled scream lodges in the valves of her heart. Hurts.

He doesn't know, he'll never know, she thinks, and she hates him all the more for that. She is crocheting her cocoon of hate with a large iron hook.

'I'm sorry,' he says.

The words are flat, without pretence. It's as though he read her mind. She drops a stitch. For a moment she forgets to hate. Opens her eyes. There are tears running down the Captain's cheek.

Outside the boys call.

'Jack! Banj! Here! Over here!'

Their fresh broken voices remind her of another time.

'I don't want it to end like this,' says the Captain.

He is thinking that the man who can modify his tactics in relation to his opponents may be called a heaven-born Captain. He needs to talk to his wife.

> 'Joan. It doesn't make sense. No-one seems to be able to tell me anything. Not really. They say they know he's dead. But they haven't found him.'

The Captain looks at her then as though he can see. And she forgets that he can't.

'Joan, they haven't found his body!'

The Captain hears hope catch on his wife's breath. The hope that Tim's not dead. Her breathing comes shallow and fast.

He doesn't want her to hope too much. But he needs her to be strong. Grow roots and have a thousand branches.

She looks at the Captain perched on the edge of the bed. Knows there is more he has to say.

'I can't leave it to them Joan.'

She lets him struggle to find the words for why.

'He's our son.'

Feelings swell in her. Choke any possibility of speech. He's never said that before. The boys outside go home for tea.

'See ya Banj!'

'Hey don't forget that stuff tomorrow.'

'Whatda' you think I am?'

'Get out!'

'Have a good one.'

The day is dying. Joan loses herself in the long shadows that are cast across the bedroom.

'I'll come with you,' she hears herself say. 'We'll look together.'

Dusk turns to night and the room becomes dark. The Captain feels for her hand. They stay like that, for a long time.

Tim wakes in the middle of the afternoon.

Heavy rain thrumming on the straw roof. Again Aik has woken before him. Tim tries to sit. Every muscle hurts.

—It's me who needs a stretcher.

He feels like shit.

After Tim and Aik eat, U Yewada takes them to meet his cousin. She is very old, shrunken by time. Bedridden. The woman with her is quick to stand when they enter.

She bows so low before U Yewada, Tim thinks she will fall over. U Yewada makes her stand straight. Relaxes her. Makes her laugh. Only then, having cleared the canvas, does U Yewada greet his cousin. Taking her hands between his and touching his forehead to hers. Tim hoods his eyes, looks at the ground. The blessing is formal, the feeling intimate; private.

U Yewada sits by his cousin's side. Her carer brings them pickled tea. It is strong, the sweetness comes later. When U Yewada introduces Tim and Aik she looks at them for the first time. Until then, Tim does not think she knew they were there. But he is wrong. Her eyes are alive, sharp with consciousness that is wise enough not to have to be polite.

When she speaks U Yewada leans close to catch her words. They talk for a long time. Late afternoon shadows forewarn night. Tim feels himself becoming restless. He is not quite sure why he and the Boy are here. He's sure there is something he should be doing. They should leave soon. Tim sips his tea in an effort to swallow his impatience. Suddenly U Yewada's cousin looks up. Signals for Tim to come closer.

He does. She examines him with her sharp eyes. Then touches his face like a child. And Tim realises she has never seen such a white person in her whole life. He smiles. She smiles. And then she blesses him. Makes him bow his head and makes a prayer.

Tim looks at U Yewada out of the corner of his eye. He really thinks they should be going soon.

> '*Di thu-nge-har kalay ta yoa loh bae. Thu sait choke htee nai ya mae.*'

The old woman's words sing. U Yewada laughs.

'She says you are too old to be impatient like a child. That when you are older impatience becomes temper.' Tim feels the heat of a blush. This satisfies U Yewada's cousin. She grunts her approval. Tells U Yewada to pass her the small wooden chest beside her bed. He does. She wears the key around her neck on faded blessing cords, grey, no longer white. She rummages through the box. Finds what she is looking for. Lays some papers on her lap. Relocks the box. U Yewada puts it back beside the bed.

Nailing Tim with her eyes she hands him the folded papers.

'A map!' Tim can't believe it.

Hurriedly he unfolds the nineteen-fifties map of Burma, lays it open on the floor.

'We are here,' says U Yewada, pointing over Tim's shoulder to a hand-drawn dot which marks the small village.

Tim looks up at the old woman. 'Thank you,' he says.

She nods once, leans back and closes her eyes. Her mind is strong. But her body is weak. Aik comes and squats beside Tim.

Looking at the map on the floor in front of him, at the line of the Salween River that marks the natural border between Thailand and Burma, cutting in so close to the village where they are, Tim feels excited. As though some pall has been lifted from him; some curse. He has a point of reference. Knows where he is in relation to other things. Will no longer be walking blind.

The words 'SHAN STATE' are printed in English above the dot that marks the village. Thailand is just across the river.

'We're so close,' says Tim, his finger tracing the line of the Salween.

'You'll make the river by morning.'

'*Ta-pyi-daw doh di-lan-go uway-mae. Lone-chone-yay ah-twe sait-nae-nae cha ya dae?*' Aik asks a question.

U Yewada tells him what he can.

'*Ko-daw lae pya-tha-nar mashi lout phu loh htin-bar dae.*'

Tim wonders what they're saying. Somehow he understands U Yewada will not be going with them.

'You're not coming?' he asks.

'No. It is better you and Aik go alone from here. The SLORC are stationed in all the villages along the river.'

The old woman speaks, her eyes still closed.

'*Buddha-yet gon-daw-koe-bar go yin-hma pipe hta yin an-da-yae kinn bay-shinn pyi ta-phet-kann go yao par lait mae.*'

'She says if you keep The Nine Attributes of the Buddha in your heart, you will reach the other side with no danger.'

Tim nods. He's not at all sure he can remember them all.

He thinks how he and the Boy have nearly come full circle.

—Almost a perfect freehand circle.

—Soon the ends will meet.

There's only a finger space between them and the river.

Squatting under the headman's house, with the chickens, U Yewada gives both Tim and Aik detailed instructions. Firstly about the route they should take. There is much discussion about this between U Yewada and Aik. And secondly about a cave above the river. A water spirit cave, where no-one goes and they can rest.

'From the river Ban Ruk Thai is two nights' walk. You cannot make it in one night. So wait until night has settled before you try and cross. Hurrying will not get you to freedom sooner. It will get you killed.'

U Yewada has pinned Tim. In his mind the river is the border. But it's not.

—'Fool Youth.'

Tim thinks the Lamas named him well. Lets the galloping of impatience slow. Notices the clouds, dark with night, edged with pink.

'How do we cross the river?' he asks.

'Swim!'

This was not exactly the answer Tim had been expecting.

'Swim?'

He thought there'd be a boat.

'Can you swim?'

'Of course I can swim!'

'Good. Aik cannot swim.'

Tim stares in disbelief. How the fuck is he supposed to get Aik across the river if he can't swim? There's not exactly time to teach him.

U Yewada hands Tim a long coil of rope.

'The river will be swollen,' he says. 'It will be hard for Aik. Perhaps you can cross first. Tie the rope to a tree on this side of the river. Carry it across with you. Tie it to a tree on the other side. This will make it easier for him. Many people cross the river like this.'

Tim's not sure it's going to be that simple. U Yewada explains to Aik who takes it in with a furrowed brow. Tim wishes he could talk with Aik.

—Maybe one day.

Is just a thought. Tim knows he's no good at languages. Three years of Tibetan classes and all he could do was order momos and thumba to go. Tim holds out his hand, a gesture to seal their undertaking. The Boy shakes his hand like a man, and each sees in the other's eyes, the reflection of his own fear. Boy or man.

A girl brings cha. The headman comes, offers cigarettes. Aik smokes. Tim finds himself thinking the Boy's too young to smoke. He can't believe he thought that.

—Old enough to die. But not to smoke.

The fifties are lodged in him, even though he thinks of himself as a child of the sixties.

—No wonder I'm fucked.

Looking out, as the last rays of the sun illuminate the tree tops, Tim lets go puritanism.

—If Vera lets Mischa drink orange juice when he eats, it's not going to kill him.

And Tim is struck by a flash of insight.

He's just like his father. He's been as dogmatic about his beliefs as his father has always been about his. As unyielding. As right. Remembering them arguing, Tim can see it for the first time, how similar they are. Red-faced. Heels dug in. Neither prepared to give ground.

The worst of his father's characteristics have seeded in him. In trying so hard to be different from his father, he has become just like him. Tim gets the giggles. Shares them with the sky. His eccentricities are middle class.

U Yewada comes and stands beside him, casts his eyes across the horizon. Tim wipes laughter from his eyes. In the almost dark he hears himself ask.

'What happened in Burma, Ka Daw? You had democracy. Aung San Sui Kyi was voted in.'

'General Saw Maung owned the army,' says U Yewada without taking his eyes from the horizon.

Tim knows there's more.

'Nothing in Burma is what it appears,' Tim says, quoting U Yewada back at himself.

'Why didn't the UN and ASAT intervene? Why didn't they place economic sanctions on Burma? Refuse to recognise the military junta?!'

Tim's questions have got away from him. They come in a rush.

'Refuse to deal with anyone but the democratically elected government?!'

U Yewada laughs. Tim thinks he's laughing at him.

'Why didn't they indeed? That question, I think, is the key.'

U Yewada breathes in deep as though breathing in his country.

'There are over one hundred different peoples living in Burma,' he says.

His gesture encompasses them all.

'To the north we're flanked by communism. To the south by capitalism. Governments don't want people to know what goes on in Burma.'

'Why not?' the question escapes from Tim.

U Yewada does not look at him.

'Opium is making someone very rich,' he says. 'And it isn't the Burmese.'

The sun drops behind the mountain opposite. In a single breath night falls. Casts a shadow across U Yewada's face. Veils the detail of him. Exposes his anger.

'There are other resources too,' he says. 'My country is being plundered.'

—Plunder.

The word sits in Tim. A word from history. On the opposite ridge a logging scar is cast silver by moonlight. Tim thought the world had changed.

He looks at U Yewada. Sees anger soften into sadness. When U Yewada speaks it is as though he were talking to himself.

'Between so many different peoples of Burma there is real hate. Hate from here.'

U Yewada holds his gut.

'Karen hate Mon. Wa, Lahu. Shan, Burmen. These are old hates. It is easy to fuel suspicions. To spread the cancer.'

Tim remembers the black Buddha. The cancer.

'This is the reality of Burma,' says U Yewada. 'But I have a hope.'

A certain stillness comes over him.

'There is an old Burmen story. Many years ago there was a grandfather with many grandsons. The grandsons were not united. They were always arguing with each other, fighting.

'One day the grandfather called all his grandsons to him, and said, "Please, bring one stick everyone, to me."

'And just as he had asked, each of his grandsons brought him one stick. The grandfather organised all the sticks together in a bundle and tried to break them. He could not. Then he took one stick and broke it easily and he explained.

'"If you are alone, someone can break you easily. If you

have unity, you cannot be broken because you are many."'

U Yewada smiles then.

'This is true Burmese culture,' he says. 'This is my hope for Burma.'

Tim swallows to keep feeling down.

Before they leave, U Yewada makes prayers over their feet, their heads, their map. He gives them each a parcel of rice and a small packet of sweet biscuits. Tim stares at the packet, machine packed, shop bought, Thai. He's never going to see U Yewada again. He looks up at the old monk.

'Thank you,' is all he finds to say.

He doesn't have any other words.

The rest of what he's feeling is in the way he takes the moment in hand. Gestures that Aik should lead the way. Aik shakes his head. Tim mimes that Aik has better eyes than him. That he is old. Almost makes Aik smile.

The Captain wakes next morning to the smell of cooking. His wife is already up, dressed, and in the kitchen.

'I thought we should have a good breakfast,' she says. He can smell the orange juice, the coffee. She is making French toast.

'Yes. That's a good idea,' he says.

He still has sleep about him. She slides their plates onto the kitchen table.

'Here,' she says and passes him a knife and fork. She always does it the same way, touching the side of his hand, so he knows where the cutlery is, never has to search.

'Forty-two years,' he says, touching her hand gently before taking the cutlery.

Her nod is a small sound caged in the back of her throat.

Tim, she thinks and her heart hurts. The Captain knows. Maybe we'll find him, are the words in his head. But he can't say them.

'I should phone Mischa. Tell him what we're doing,' is the best he can do.

His words mean a lot. Joan swallows the sentiment that rises. Later, some time in the future, on a warm night she will kiss him, and the fractured pieces of their fairytale will come together.

'Mischa!'

Vera calls from the hall.

'It's John!'

Mischa comes out of his room. He heard the phone ring. He's not sure who John is. Vera holds the phone out for him.

'Your grandfather!' her eyes underline the word.

Mischa takes the phone. He's not sure he likes this.

'Hello?' he says, tentative. He doesn't remember the Captain ever phoning him before.

The voice on the other end is kinder than he remembers. First the Captain asks him how he's bearing up, as though it really matters. Mischa never thought his grandfather really liked him much. And then he says, he hasn't been doing too well. That he thinks the whole thing is bloody horrible and doesn't make sense. Asks Mischa what he thinks. Mischa says he doesn't understand any of it.

'Well neither do I,' says the Captain.

Now Mischa is listening. Even his grandfather, a man, a Captain is struggling.

'Your grandmother and I think we should go to Thailand and try and sort things out,' he says. 'What do you think?'

'Can you do that?' asks Mischa. Hope in his voice.

'Yes,' says the Captain, and he hears himself add quickly, 'I don't know if we'll find him Mischa. But we will find out what happened.'

The Captain's stomach knots.

'One way or another.'

He doesn't want to let his grandson down.

'Is that OK?'

Mischa nods. Then remembers he's on the telephone.

'Yeah. I think that's good.'

His grandfather's going to find out what happened. He doesn't have to do it by himself. Doesn't have to know. Doesn't have to be the keeper.

Being the best person you can.

Tim thinks about this as he follows close on Aik's heels. The night holds pockets of unseasonal cool. Cloud hangs low. There is no moon. Here and now, Tim is being the best person he can; for Aik. He wonders why he didn't do it for his son.

—Choice.

He blocks that voice.

He doesn't want to know. Doesn't want to deal with that. Reckons some things are better left alone. But the strange night that draws from the earth its humours, to rise as serpents of mist, seems to amplify the voice. Until Tim can no longer block it out.

—Choice.

Logic tells Tim that this omission of choice has nothing to do with Mischa. How much he loves him. Yet still he doesn't want to look at it. Somehow it seems to Tim to mark their relationship, stain it. That's what galls him. He draws night into his lungs. One foot in front of the other he follows Aik. In the distance there is half-hearted thunder.

—If I didn't want to be a father I should have used a condom!

He spits the thought at himself.

—In the end that's what it comes down to.

The hairs on the back of his neck rise. There's more to it than that. The jungle seems to close in on him until he can hardly breathe. He feels himself animal. Sex is in him. It's in his scent. He has no relationship with pregnancy.

The image that springs to his mind is of fish spawning. Bright coloured fish, fluorescent yellow. He can hear David Attenborough commentating.

—'They scatter their seed indiscriminately. It is up to the female to do the rest. The propagation of the species depends on this.'

A cold shiver runs down Tim's spine. Set against the dark detail of hand on rough bark, the mineral scent of soil, his own sweat, the image of fish spawning is laughable.

The path descends steeply. He grabs hold of a tree for balance and tries to cut into the wet track with the edge of his sandals. Give his feet grip.

—Just too young.

Thinks Tim, remembering himself back then. Remembering how he tried so hard to be open. Not think too much.

—I succeeded in that.

The voice of self-recrimination. He almost slips.

Even when Vera said she was pregnant he didn't really think about what it meant. How it would change things. He remembers saying to a friend it was Vera having the baby, not him, and they'd both laughed. Now the memory doesn't sit so well.

It never occurred to him that he was involved—even now his mind shies away from the word responsible—for what was happening.

Resistance is in him. In the way the muscles in his back clench. Hold feeling back from his heart. He has always held back. Resisted. Even when it came to spending time with Mischa. Not that he didn't enjoy their time together. He did. Those days were special. It was the 'should' of it he resented. The fact that he was expected to do all these things because he was suddenly somebody's Daddy. He hated that. Wanted it to be something different.

In the dark, the world is without detail, Tim is using other senses.

—It's just the way it is.

—You're somebody's Daddy.

He is Mischa's father, no-one else.

Tim has a horrible feeling that by not thinking about this stuff sooner, he has done them all a disservice. Suddenly he really wants to hold Mischa. Feels the need in the muscles of his arms. Wants to say, 'Sorry mate'. Feels a sense of urgency he's not familiar with.

—'We'll get together then Dad.'

Some things can't wait. He's been looking at the whole thing upside down.

—Everything changes.

—Not forever.

—Precious.

In his excitement, Tim slips. Catches himself with a hooked arm. Jars his shoulder. Grazes his chin against bark. Aik plants a boot, stops him from sliding further. Tim is covered in mud. It begins to rain a little. Tim can't stop smiling.

Aik puts out his hand to help him stand. Taking Aik's hand, Tim has an overwhelming desire to hug the boy. He laughs at the thought. If he did Aik would probably slit his throat. He wonders if U Yewada knew Aik was carrying a knife.

After that, they descend together. Tim with a hand on Aik's shoulder. Two weeks before, Tim would not have imagined this to be a possibility.

—Everything changes.

Tim feels a humility not familiar to him.

On the map the distance to the river may have seemed short but in reality it is a long, hard walk. They avoid villages, and well-worn tracks, in case of patrols. The closer they get to the river, the stronger Tim feels the presence of the enemy. His mind plays tricks. He sees them in shadows lurking.

—Fear.

He tells himself. He can almost taste freedom and he doesn't want to lose it.

Without warning Aik drops to the ground. Tim is down, squatting beside him, heart pounding, before he's had time to think. Aik looks at him. Undoes his boot laces. He has a stone in his shoe. Tim shrugs. Smiles. Rocks back to sit in the racing of his heart. Wonders why men don't talk about this shit. About being so scared you could piss yourself.

—It can't be good for you not talking about it.

He is thinking about his father. He must have felt like this. Scared, skittish like a rabbit. He never said a word about that stuff. Neither did his mates.

Suddenly Aik grabs hold of Tim's wrist. Squeezes a warning. They freeze. Hardly breathe. Their hearts beat like drums; too loud. Something crawls down Tim's back. He does not move.

How could he explain this? The control it takes to hold still against fear so strong it twists in your gut. Makes you think you will be sick.

—There is nothing heroic about this.

Tim understands the bond between his father and the handful of mates he served with. Knowing was hidden in their beer guts.

Tim sees a shadow moving. Black on black, like the rat he saw when he was first kidnapped, only this time it's a man. Walking towards them. Closer, closer.

—Just one man.

Tim's mind is quick to calculate the odds. He didn't even mean to do it, it's instinct. Aik stands without warning. Calls out.

'*Oo-gyi, Oo-gyi.*'

Tim's heart misses a beat. He doesn't want this for Mischa. The shadow man pauses.

'*Hey, min-doh di-mha bar loat nay dar lae?*' he answers and walks towards them.

Tim stands, caught a beat behind the action. He's going to tell Mischa about this stuff. Hopes he doesn't forget.

The man is close enough now for Tim to make out the

detail of him. He is a hunter. Armed with bows and arrows. Dressed in a lungi pulled between his legs. He carries three knives. His lips are stained with betel-nut. His eyes don't shine.

Tim nods a greeting. Is ignored.

Aik and the hunter talk a little.

The hunter shakes his head. Spits on the ground in disgust. Even Tim understands. SLORC are everywhere. After that, they beat their own path through the jungle. Keep clear of all tracks.

The sun has already begun to rise,
by the time Tim and Aik look down on the Salween. Breaking out of the jungle to look down on the river is like breaking out of a dream. Tim's body quivers with exhaustion. They are both scratched and stained. Aik stares at the river as though it were going to tell him something.

Crows call. Tim remembers home. The smell of the Murray on summer mornings when you first stagger out of your tent to piss and no-one else has stirred.

Without warning he is struck by the memory of the warm animal smell of Vera, curled in their sleeping bag, and wonders if he will ever have a partner again; a mate.

Aik tugs at his T-shirt. Points across the river. Tim looks. Rising out of the mist is a tower of sticks, perched high on a hill, on the opposite side of the river. A lookout. Tim realises from that vantage, the soldiers will have a clear view of the river once it turns.

He looks down at the water, brown with silt, already swollen with monsoon rain and flowing fast. He nearly drowned once. When he was about five. His mother hauled him out of the surf by the back of his shorts. Very humiliating.

He's never forgotten it. Had a healthy respect for water ever since. He makes himself think. Crossing, he's going to be carried down river by the current. The question is how far, and that all depends on how strong a swimmer he is. Tim thinks perhaps they should err on the side of caution and head up river quite a way before they try and cross.

Without a word Aik lowers himself over the edge of the cliff and begins to climb down. Tim follows. Trusts his hands and feet to find a way. Halfway down Tim's feet find a ledge. Aik is already edging his way along it towards a slit that weeps. The water spirit cave.

Inside the cave it's dark. Stinks of bat shit. A constant trickle of water runs along one edge to its mouth. Aik drinks. Tim drinks. Above them, the wings of bats beat the air, Tim looks up. The ceiling of the cave is high. Latticed with half a dozen skylights, where wind and rain have worn away the rock.

—Bats. Rats with wings.

Tim's glad they are clinging to the ceiling. Wishes he could shake the feeling that he was in someone's mouth. Someone old, who dribbled.

The first shouts on the river shock. Both Tim and Aik start. They edge their way to the mouth of the cave and peer out. Careful to keep hidden. SLORC soldiers have commandeered the river. Tim and Aik watch in silence. Catch glimpses of the soldiers when the mist thins.

Tim wonders if they shouldn't have planned to cross the river somewhere where it wasn't so busy. Where the river was further from the Thai border. He thinks now that would have been a more strategic move. Less predictable.

He edges his way back into the cave. Sits.

—Fuck them.

They're not going to get him.

—Not now.

When they're so close.

Tim leans back against the wall, steel cool stone. Adrenalin amplifies the sensation. He's not going to be able to sleep. He's strung too tight. A line set to snap. He's got to ease the tension. Work the line. Tim looks at Aik. The boy seems dazed.

He takes out his parcel of rice. Shows it to Aik. A suggestion they should eat. They do. It helps. Aik stops looking so chalky. And Tim realises how much he hates dried fish flakes.

Others come to the river, one at a time. Come for water. Tim only sees one boat. An old man who edges his way down river, close to the bank. Tim thinks he must be a trader. The small wooden boat is filled with boxes.

Aik does not watch the river. He sifts stones, intent. Until he has six of approximately the same size and then he begins to play. Tim watches out of the corner of his eye. Throw one stone, pick up two. Throw one stone, pick up three.

—Jacks!

Tim's got it.

When Aik wins against himself, Tim suggests they play, one against the other.

'You and me. OK?'

'OK.'

Aik hands him a stone.

The game is not exactly Jacks. Aik has drawn lines in the silted dirt of the cave floor. There's something about where you place the stones. Tim's sure Aik cheats. Keeps changing the rules. Tim is up to threes.

'Yes!'

'No.'

Aik shakes his head. Takes one stone from Tim's hand and places it back in its square.

'No way!'

They argue with gesture and few words, mime out the rules. They forget about the river. The muscles in Tim's back loosen. His ears stop ringing from listening too hard. Aik wins the first game. The second. Tim challenges a third. Outside the day grows hot. Again Tim loses. Eyeing the Boy, Tim challenges him to noughts and crosses. His manhood at stake.

Aik is quick to claim the centre square. Tim blocks him. No-one wins. The hours pass quickly. The first drops of rain fall heavy on the river in the early afternoon. A shower. No-one comes after that. Looking out across the deserted river, Tim keeps thinking about those packets of sweet biscuits. He could eat a horse. Well at least a whole leg of lamb. His mouth waters. He hasn't eaten meat for years.

He takes the packet of biscuits from his pocket. Counts them through the cellophane. Twenty thin sweet wafers. Forty biscuits. He opens the packet. Takes two. Gives two to Aik.

Aik holds up his own packet.

'Later,' says Tim and makes Aik take the biscuits. Aik puts away his packet.

The real rain starts about an hour later. Traps heat. Sends eddies of warm air into the cave. The sound lulls them. Tim has to sleep now. Leaning back against the cave wall he closes his eyes.

In his dream it is night. But it is raining. He and Aik

have found a boat. Tim is pleased they have found a boat. They fight roots and tangled marsh and try to work it toward the river. It is a tin boat. Tim wonders how a tin boat came to be here.

Suddenly they are on the river. Floating down the river. The sky is filled with stars. There is no sound except for the sound of water against the hull of the boat. And then there is the crack of the arc. The sky lights up. A tracer.

Tim looks at Aik. But Aik is Mischa. Tim is aware he has grown into a fine man.

Again there is the crack of the arc followed by the sound of water. The boy's face is blown away.

'NO!'

Tim wakes screaming. A dream, he tells himself.

—Just a dream.

The next four hours are the longest of Tim's life. Bats leave the cave in great squadrons, black against the night. He and Aik eat biscuits. They stick to the roof of Tim's mouth. He has to wash them down with water.

—Alkaline with bat shit.

He doesn't like being in the cave in the dark. There is a constant pain in his chest. A dance between fear and hope. And there is the constant sound of water. When night settles there is a quiet that falls upon the jungle. Tim hears it, or rather the hush of it. He looks at Aik. It's time. He tries a smile. He's tired of being scared. He fingers the paper of names in his pocket. Secures it for the crossing. Thinks about holding Mischa.

Leaving the cave they stay close together, move slowly, quietly. Tim thinks he can hear Aik's heart as well as his own.

Once down on the bank of the river, Tim takes the lead. They head upstream. Tim carries the rope slung across one shoulder.

The going's hard. They slip in the mud. Tim has to use his whole body to push through the tangle of jungle along the bank. He's not sure how far up river they should go. Not sure how far the current will carry him before he gets across. Not sure how strong a swimmer he is.

—Stronger than Aik.

That thought doesn't help.

The giant tree, fallen out over the river ten yards up ahead, forming a natural pier, does, however.

—Yes!

—It's a sign.

Things are going their way. Tim pushes through the jungle with renewed vigour. He's been worried the rope wouldn't be long enough. Wouldn't reach.

He lays a hand on the upturned roots as though simply reaching the tree were a minor victory. He beams a smile at Aik.

Aik doesn't share his sentiment. He just looks shit scared. Tim realises he's always liked celebrating minor victories. Didn't see the point in hanging out for the big ones. He uncoils the rope. Ties one end around his waist, and carrying the coil, steps towards the river.

Aik taps him on the shoulder. Holds up the unopened packet of biscuits. Tim had completely forgotten about the other packet of biscuits. Aik hadn't. They squat. Eat, ten biscuits each. Fuel for the swim. They don't wait half an hour.

'OK,' whispers Tim, slipping into the water.

Aik tugs at his T-shirt.

Tim glares.

—What now!

Aik makes the sign of a snake swimming, then biting.

—I really need to know that right now.

Tim makes himself smile. Turns back to the river. Edges his way along the trunk of the tree. Ties the other end of the rope to a solid fork, above the water line. Takes one last look at Aik. Thumbs up, and dives in.

The water is cold. The current strong. Especially in the centre. Tim has to fight it. Use all his strength. He's carried down river nearly twenty yards. Realises he's not going to make it before the river turns. Suddenly the rope around his waist pulls tight. He'd forgotten about that.

The drag of the rope threatens to pull him back to the shore he has just left. Now he has to swim against the current. Fight even harder.

—Fuck them.

—Not now!

—They're not going to get me now.

Anger gives him strength.

He takes a breath and dives down. He was always a better swimmer under water. He feels himself moving forward. Feels the pull of the current on the rope around his waist. Comes up for air. Dives again. Comes up for air. His feet touch stones that slip beneath his toes. Almost there. The rope pulls tight. He's got to head upstream.

—Just a few more feet upstream.

He dives. Uses his whole body. Comes up for air again. Hurls himself against the current. An ungainly fish. His feet find ground. He tugs at the rope. Drags it with him as he wades upstream. His eyes search out Aik on the opposite bank. He's there. A shadow by the tree. Aik waves. He's made it. He waves. The labouring of his lungs tells him he only just made it.

Tim unties the rope from his waist. Finds a small but sturdy tree on the edge of the bank. Struggles to pull the rope taut across the river. Ties it off. Knot after knot. Three knots. That's the best he can do. He looks at his handiwork before turning and giving Aik the thumbs up.

Aik lowers himself into the water. Makes his way out along the trunk of the fallen tree towards the rope. Tim watches. His heart has stopped beating.

Aik takes hold of the rope with both hands. His feet lose touch with the ground. He kicks them out behind him. It's instinct. The current pushes him hard up against the rope. Draws him under. Hand over hand he pulls himself forward. Struggles to keep his head above water. Take a clear breath. Struggles but does not let go of the rope.

By the time Aik is halfway across the river, Tim is already waist-deep, heading out along the line of the rope. His grip, when he reaches the Boy, is firm. He drags him from the river. Aik collapses on the muddy bank, where the soil is different. Wipes water from his face. Looks at Tim and smiles.

Tim has never seen him smile before. It makes him look younger.

—Look his age.

Feeling threatens.

—'Boys don't cry.'

He smiles. They shake hands. Mates, thinks Tim.

Different soil. Different smell.

The jungle is different on this side of the river. Tim feels humbled. He's only just worked out how much he didn't like himself before. He looks over his shoulder. Aik is still smiling. Only now his eyes have caught on.

The mountainous jungle along the border soon drains from both Tim and Aik all newly found inspiration. They hear grain being hulled. The rhythmic pounding rises from the valleys. On the outskirts of villages they see makeshift shelters. Housing for refugees or soldiers? There are large tracts of jungle being logged along the border. Datsun 120 Ys stand dwarfed with three-ton loads of timber. Tim can't believe his eyes. Thinks if he ever buys another car, that's the one for him. He and Aik steer clear of all villages and logging camps.

As the night draws on, Tim feels like he's fighting his body all the way. They have to stop often. When Tim's stomach begins to cramp they have to stop for him to shit. He can't believe the timing of it. Doesn't need this now. They're nearly there.

When the cramps ease they walk on. Tim wonders if they've crossed the border yet.

—No, that's tomorrow.

It won't mean anything until they walk into Ban Ruk Thai anyway.

—No signposts in the jungle.

Tim's trying to make himself think about something other than the pain. But it keeps grabbing his attention. He has broken into a sweat. He can feel it. When he shits again it's blood and mucus. He's not feeling good.

'Jesus!' He swears through clenched teeth. The cramps are aberrant.

'Not nooow.'

Amoebas. He's had them before in Nepal.

Tim bites his knee in response to the pain in his gut.

Fight pain with pain. When the cramp passes he looks up. A moment of peace. Aik is worried. The smile has gone from his face. He looks lost. Tim pulls himself together. Stands. Feels as weak as a baby. Or as if someone had just driven a semi through his gut.

'Bad timing eh? Enough to give you the shits,' he says and smiles weakly at his own pun.

They walk on slowly. When a cramp comes they pause, Aik often holding Tim, helping him so that he can curl into the cramp. After a few hours the cramps begin to ease. Warning cramps die away, without ever growing teeth. Tim waits, nothing. He straightens, nothing. He shrugs. Aik understands he's doing better. Smiles again. Tim makes himself keep walking.

They stop just on dawn. Find a ledge of rock they can shelter under. Tim curls in under the ledge. He has to sleep. He is incredibly tired.

He wakes, feeling much better. His bum is in a puddle of water. It's raining. Beside him Aik is asleep. A boy with his mouth open. A boy, thinks Tim, who didn't fall asleep until he covered them both in leaves and grasses. Camouflaged them.

Tim is incredibly thirsty. He has to drink. He opens his mouth under the runoff from the ledge. He never knew cold earthy water could taste so good.

—One more night.

The thought grabs him.

This is it. Their last obstacle and then the nightmare really will be over. Tim feels raw, every sense heightened. It's not a pleasant feeling. Waves of hope and fear play with him. Take him out of his body. Take him away from where he is, sitting with his bum in a puddle of water, feeling quite good. Take him into the future, a place he cannot go yet.

He remembers Rimpoche saying,

—'If you are worried and there is something you can do about the problem, do it. If you are worried and there is nothing you can do, stop worrying.'

Worrying is not going to help either him or the boy.

Tim closes his eyes. Makes himself breathe deeply. Exhales stale air. Cleans out his body, his mind. Watches his breath come easily then. Unforced. He sits like that for quite a while. Not racing to get onto the next thing. The real practice, the visualisation. He realises he's never done that before. Sat in being.

—It's OK.

He cuts the thought. Dedicates this simple practice for the benefit of all beings. Suddenly a great sadness wells up inside of him.

—So much suffering.

Wind plays with the rain. The smell of earth is strong. The boy rolls over in his sleep. The jungle is peaceful. The rain peaceful. There is an uprush of joy at this simplicity. Tim watches it settle.

—'Now what to do?'

Rimpoche's words are in his head. Tim sits with them. Realises he is smiling. He is happy. Happy is not a big thing. It is small. The black between his shoulders clears. He imagines himself filled with light.

It is late afternoon when Aik stirs. He is excited. Tim can see it in his eyes.

'Ban Ruk Thai,' he says.

Impatient for night. Tim nods.

'Ban Ruk Thai.'

'Tim OK,' says Aik.

He has pulled Tim's name from the air. Feeling catches somewhere between Tim's heart and his throat. Most uncomfortable.

'Yeah,' is a whisper.

Walking through the jungle, in the dark, for the last time. Tim sees himself and Aik as two single brushstrokes on paper; yellow and red. He hasn't seen things in colour for a long time.

It is Aik who spots the road to Ban Ruk Thai, cutting through the hills. They look down on the thin dirt line to freedom, from a vantage high in the jungle.

'You sure?' asks Tim.

Aik nods. They make their way carefully towards the road.

Now Tim really is shit scared. His palms are sweating. And he feels a real sense of threat. He's not sure why. Finding the road means they're in Thailand. They've made it. Everything should be simple now. But it doesn't feel that way. Tim's mouth is dry and he's scared. His sixth sense is working overtime. He follows Aik's lead. They crouch hidden, at the edge of the jungle, near the road.

Day begins to lighten the sky. Dawn is a strange reality when one has been up all night. Cows round the bend in the road. Head towards them. Towards Ban Ruk Thai. Soon the strange encouragements of their cowherds, the rhythmic beating of sticks on ground, can be heard. Farmers rise early.

The cows pass. The farmers pass. There are three of

them. Aik tugs at Tim's sleeve and steps out onto the road. They join behind the group of farmers herding their cows into Ban Ruk Thai. The farmers pay them no attention. They amble. Tim and Aik amble, a few feet behind. Others join them. Appear out of the jungle, booty for market strapped to their backs, carried on their heads.

When the mist clears Tim sees a lookout in the distance. Understands. He and Aik will seem like farmers. Nothing out of the ordinary.

'Ban Ruk Thai,' says Aik, pointing at the lookout.

Tim smiles. Puts a hand on Aik's shoulder.

'Food,' he says.

And mimes eating. Aik almost laughs.

'*Hoat-tae, bite-pyae ya dot mae*,' he says.

Also miming eating. He is hungry.

It is not long before the road widens and the jungle thins. Soon they will be walking into the village. Walking into Ban Ruk Thai. To freedom. They round a bend and there is a house. Soon there are others. They've made it.

—It's over!

Tim notices a man watching from outside his shack. He stands poised above his ablutions. Aik locks eyes with him, keeps walking.

The man walks to the roadside as he dries his face. Pauses casual, at the post that marks the entrance to his shack. As they near, he bows his head almost imperceptibly.

Aik slows, wanders over. Tim takes his lead from Aik.

'*Bar-mar lar kwa?*' asks the man as he spits betel-nut juice into the open drain that runs along the roadside.

Aik nods.

The man is Burmese. Has picked Aik as Burmese.

They stand gathered at the post. Aik and the man talk.

Aik is shy, he looks mostly at the ground. Plays with a stone with his foot.

The man shakes his head. Spits betel-nut juice at the ground near Tim's feet. Lifts his gaze, and pins Tim with a look that makes him think of bloodied chickens, throats freshly cut.

Tim tries a smile. The attempt is half-hearted, his smile lopsided.

'*Kya-naw doh go ku-nyi bar. Thu, thu-nai-gnan pyan-ya-mae,*' says Aik.

Lifting his gaze to meet the man's. He means what he is saying. This much Tim knows.

Again the man shakes his head and looks at Tim.

Tim had thought that threat would be a thing of the past once they reached Thailand. Now looking into the Burmese stranger's eyes, he is not so sure. There is the warning of danger in the yellowing white of his eyes.

'*Aye,*' he says suddenly, '*Ywa-guang-zaung net za-gar pyaw pot. Nga-naut lai khe.*'

And signals that they should follow.

They leave the main road. Cut through foot-beaten pathways that lead between houses. Led away from the Thai border police lookout, on the hill, overlooking the village. Tim is confused. Wonders why they are not going there. Once they get there the nightmare will be over.

The man stops. Points.

There is a bamboo house at the end of the path. The headman's house. Tim had forgotten about custom. The man leaves them then without a word. Heads back the way they have just come. Watching him go, Tim thinks you would never know it was him who had shown them the way.

The headman is Thai. He seems more surprised by Aik's appearance at his door, than Tim's. Tim wonders why. Can't help feeling he's missing something. The headman listens solemnly to Aik. Tells them to wait. Disappears around the back of his house. Tim hears the sound of washing. An old woman gives them tea and a banana.

Tim would not have believed a banana could taste so good. He looks at Aik. Smiles.

—The nightmare's nearly over.

Aik is not smiling. The banana is good but he is not smiling.

When the headman appears again, he is wearing a short-sleeved white shirt.

—'Glow Weave', wrinkle free.

—Civilisation.

Tim still has issues with men and shirts and the quest to eliminate any human wrinkle.

People notice them following the headman. Stare. This is it, thinks Tim. They're in the open now. He tells himself, it's over. That he should feel ecstatic.

—Fucking ecstatic.

But he doesn't. Neither does Aik.

Aik has locked himself down into his nuggetty bird-boy body. Tim thinks he understands. He is uncomfortable being visible, when he's become so good at hiding.

When they present themselves to the Thai border police, there is much excitement. They have Tim's picture. Issued by the Australian Embassy. Messages are sent. They are very proud of themselves for finding him. That is how it seems to Tim. The Thai police captain asks him many questions in broken English. Tim doesn't say much. He is careful. Says they are hungry and sick. Says the boy, Aik, saved him, that is all.

Aik is treated with suspicion. Made to sit. Asked questions. The headman translates. The border police don't speak Burmese. Tim hadn't thought of that. The practicalities of custom.

Tim is given black tea with sugar. Aik is not. Tim is offered a cigarette.

'No thanks,' he says. 'But the boy might like one.' And he points to Aik.

The policeman in his camouflage uniform ignores him. Both gesture and words. It is as if the suggestion was never made.

'They have a doctor for you now Mr Rhyder,' says the police captain. Pointing to a young Thai policeman standing in the doorway. Tim doesn't think he looks much of a doctor.

'You go now please,' says the captain.

'What about Aik? What about the boy?'
The captain takes Tim's arm to help him stand.

Policeman will take you,' he says, avoiding Tim's question. Tim holds his ground.

'The boy has malaria. He needs to see a doctor.'

'He will. He will,' says the captain.
Tim looks across the room at Aik sitting in a straight-backed chair. A stranger in another man's office.

'Just a few more questions,' says the captain.
Here Tim is a guest.

'Ask me more questions then,' says Tim.
He has the weight of his passport behind him. He's just not sure how much weight that carries.

BURMESE TRANSLATIONS

Page 66
'*Ma-nay-nya ga bar dway ait-matt matt lae?*'
What did you dream last night?

Page 67
'*Hey! htaung-thar dway, hta-hta.*'
Hey, all prisoners get up, get up.

Page 102
'*Hey-kaung-dway, thwar-loh-ya pyi. Thwar dot!*'
Hey, all of you can go now. Go!

'*Thu-go ah-khan-htae pait lai tot.*'
Lock him up.

Page 136
'*Ha, ah-thet-shin yet shi thay da bae. Kaung-dae. Kaung-dae.*'
Ha, you guys are still alive. Good. Good.

Page 161
'*Kyay-zue tin bar dae.*'
Thank you.

Page 179
'*Hint-inn, ma-yut phu.*'
No. We are not going to stop.

Page 180
'*Thwar! Thwar!*'
Go! Go!

Page 185
'*Kya-naw ah-phe har di-sit-tat ko taw-hlan pyi ah-thet sone khe ya tae so dar thu-go pyaw pya pay bar.*'
Please tell him that my father died of resisting this military.

'*Ah-khu kya-naw lut-lat pyi. Ah-phe tu thar phit aung jo-zar mae. Thu-loh ah-thet-pay yin pay ya pa zae.*'
I am free now. I'll try to be a father-like son even if I have to die like him by resisting this military.

'*Ah-thet za-dae ya dar htet shin-tan taw-hlan ya dar po ah-date-pae shi mae htin dae.*'
Staying alive and resisting is more meaningful than death.

'*Kya-naw jo-zar hma bar.*'
I will try my best.

Page 192
'*Di thu-nge-har kalay ta yoa loh bae. Thu sait choke htee nai ya mae.*'

He acts (is) like a child. He must control his mind and temper.

Page 194
'*Ta-pyi-daw doh di-lan-go uway-mae. Lone-chone-yah ah-twe sait-nae-nae cha ya dae.*'
We will choose this route. It is a bit safer.

'*Ko-daw lae pya-tha nar mashi lout phu loh htin-bar dae.*'
I also think there should not be any problem.

'*Buddha-yet gon-daw-koe-bar go yin-hma pipe hta yin an-da-yae kinn bay-shinn pyi ta-phet-kann go yao par lait mae.*'
If you remember the Nine Attributes of Buddha in your heart, you will reach safely to the other side of the river.

Page 205
'*Oo-gyi, Oo-gyi.*'
Uncle, uncle.

'*Hey, min-doh di-mha bar loat nay dar lae?*'
Hey, what are you doing here?

Page 218
'*Hoat-tae, bite-pyae ya dot mae.*'
Yes, we are going to have a meal.

'*Ba-mar lar kwa?*'
Are you Burmese?

Page 219

'*Kya-naw doh go ku-nyi bar. Thu, thu-nai-gnan pyan-ya-mae.*'
Please help us. He needs to go back to his country.